A Different Way of Life

20 short stories
all set on and around the
Isle of Wight

by

Jan Wright

Jan Wright was born and raised on the Isle of Wight, a popular holiday destination off the South Coast of England. She has been writing for many years and her short stories have appeared in many of the popular weekly women's magazines in the UK. Her stories have also appeared in magazines in both Europe and Australia.

Versions of some of these stories have been published in various magazines in the past but have all been reworked and updated.

All Profits from the sale of this book are going to the Island's local hospice – Mountbatten Isle of Wight.

© Jan Wright 2025

The stories contained in this book are all works of fiction. Names, characters, places and events are either products of the author's imagination or are used fictitiously. Any resemblance to actual persons, living or dead, is purely coincidental.

All rights reserved.

No part of this book may be reproduced, stored in a retrieval system or transmitted in any form, electronic, mechanical, photocopying, recording or otherwise without the written permission of the author.

*For Aisha, Beth and Rob
with all my love xxx*

*And for my Mum & Dad –
I wish they could have seen this.*

Contents

A Different Way of Life 7
The Swinging Sixties... 27
Leeway, Dead Reckoning and Estimated Position 43
Too Young.. 57
It's a Crime 69
Unrealistic Expectations 83
Letting Go.. 101
The Holiday 111
Touched By The Moon.. 117
Tinsel and Turkey.. 125
The Perfect Place... 143
Mayday, Mayday, Mayday!... 155
Golden Opportunity... 161
Nauseatingly Nautical 173
You Can't Have It All 185
The End of an Era.. 199
In Need of Some First Aid... 213
A Lack of Maternal Instinct... 221
Flying Free 241
Surprise Surprise! 255
Acknowledgements 269

A Different Way of Life

I had the row with Alex the same day as my mother broke her ankle. Not that the two things were connected. I mean Alex wasn't to blame for Mum's accident, even if he was responsible for every other problem in my life.

I arrived at the hospital to find Mum in a complete flap. Not about her ankle you understand, she wasn't the sort to worry about herself. She was fretting about her best friend, Rose.

'What am I going to do?' Mum sobbed all over me. 'I have to go to the Isle of Wight tomorrow. Rose is relying on me and I can't let her down.'

'Mum, there's no way you can go tomorrow,' I said as gently as I could. 'Rose will understand that even you, as clever as you are, can't magic your ankle better.' Which made her sob even harder, so I fished around in my handbag and found her a clean tissue.

It was ironic really, if she hadn't fallen down those steps, I'd now be the one crying all over her. Well, I had just told Alex where he could shove his job, his engagement ring and our future together. Which left me unemployed, alone and, if I was honest, feeling pretty damned awful.

I'd stormed out of his office and was about to drive over to Mum's for tea, sympathy and some advice, when I had the call from the hospital. But I could hardly dump my problems on her now, not given the circumstances.

'I'm sure Rose can get someone else to help in the shop,' I said, while trying to smile encouragingly.

'Of course she can,' Mum replied. 'But you know full well that I'm going there to give Rose emotional support. She's very nervous about selling everything off and closing down her business.'

Mum and Rose had been friends forever. While Rose was a little older than Mum, they'd lived on the same street and, from what I'd been told, Rose got Mum into all sorts of mischief, although Rose insists Mum was the bad influence. Whichever it was, they stayed in touch after Mum's family moved off the Island when Mum was sixteen.

I was born about ten years later, and my father didn't stay around long so there was never much money. However, I grew up spending every summer on the Isle of Wight, all thanks to darling Rose. She'd ended up taking over her family's beachside shop, and we always stayed with her in the flat above it. It wasn't a huge flat, but it had three bedrooms and from my tiny one I had a perfect view of the sea. Plus, I was free to walk across the road and play on the beach all day long. It was a fantastic change from the dusty, noisy city I called home.

I thought it sad Rose was giving up the shop her grandfather had opened ten years before she'd been born. But she was now almost sixty and fed-up with PAYE, VAT, and the ever-changing rules and regulations. She wanted to shut up shop, but she didn't - if you know what I mean!

I hadn't seen her shop for about fifteen years, but I'd seen Rose every winter when she stayed with Mum. I loved her dearly and hated to think of her having to face this without Mum's help. I looked at Mum lying in bed; she now had my stepdad, her sister, a stepdaughter-in-law and several good neighbours, so she wasn't short of people to help look after her.

Rose didn't have anyone, and I knew she didn't like my boyfriend much, which might help given my present circumstances. I needed to get away from Alex, so where better to run to than the Isle of Wight.

'I'll go and help Rose,' I announced.

'Oh Jen, that's a sweet suggestion, but I can't see Alex agreeing to it,' Mum replied.

'Alex can manage fine without me,' I said. Well, he could certainly make decisions without bothering to talk to me. I still couldn't believe how much money he'd borrowed to buy into some dodgy business deal with his new mate Des.

'But Jen, this is an investment for our future,' Alex had told me earlier. 'In a year's time, Des and I will have made a fortune. Just think, we'll be able to buy a house without a mortgage.'

'And pigs might fly!'

'Where's your spirit of adventure?'

'Gone missing with your common sense. Alex, have you looked at these figures?' I asked, waving several bits of paper at him.

'Of course I have. Des has accounted for all contingencies.'

'No, he hasn't. What about...?' I'd then given him a long list of expenditure items that Des had conveniently missed. 'Why didn't you let me look at this before you committed the money?'

'I wanted to surprise you.'

'Well, you certainly did that.' And so the row had gone on. Alex was upset that I didn't believe he could make us millionaires overnight, and I was upset that he couldn't see Des for the conman he so obviously was. Alex was always a bit impulsive, but he'd changed since he'd met Des. Money had become an obsession.

Half of me wanted to ring Alex as soon as I left the hospital, but the other half knew it wouldn't help. We both needed some time to think, which was why escaping to the Isle of Wight was a good idea. Rose seemed to like it too, although she was concerned about Mum.

'She'll be better once she knows you're happy about me coming over,' I said.

'And you're sure Alex doesn't mind losing you from the office for so long?' Rose asked.

I wasn't sure about anything, but if he had a problem he could always call his mate. Des, I was sure, was a lot better at creative accounting than I'd ever be.

That evening, I packed my car before crawling off to bed and finally giving way to the tears I'd been holding back. Alex and I were supposed to be getting married in nine months' time. Did I really want to cancel the wedding? The answer was no, I just wanted my old Alex back, the one I'd fallen in love with. Assuming that man really existed and wasn't just a figment of my imagination. Could it be he'd always been like this, and I just hadn't noticed?

The next morning it took me nearly two hours to drive to Portsmouth, and it wasn't until the ferry sailed out of the harbour that I felt myself start to relax. I stood on deck with the sun on my back and watched as the boat cut through the calm blue waters. It was peaceful despite the sky being full of noisy seagulls. I envied the way they soared so high and free, and I wondered if life looked less complicated from up there, because it sure looked a mess from down here.

The first thing that struck me as I carefully manoeuvred my way off the ferry was the amount of traffic. There were coaches and huge supermarket lorries everywhere, and the line of cars went on forever. Funny, but I didn't remember this tranquil little haven having so many traffic jams and one-way systems. It was only about twelve miles to Rose's, but it took me ages to get there. I didn't know the way and the Island roads were narrow and extremely bumpy – it was a world away from the motorways and city roads I was used to.

Everything had looked very different when I'd been in the back of Rose's car all those years ago, but I did recognise Godshill and its thatched cottages. As I drove through the village, I could picture us all walking to the top of the hill to visit the church, and afterwards eating strawberries and cream in the tea gardens.

It couldn't be true, but in my memory we'd had bright sunshine all through those holidays, and my sandcastles had been huge, the sea warm and each day had lasted a week.

At least the seafront, when I eventually found it, looked vaguely familiar and I had no problem finding Rose's, mainly because the place hadn't changed a bit. It was one of those touristy shops stuffed full of things nobody needs, but everyone buys. As I looked in the window, the years disappeared. The tea towels and perpetual calendars looked exactly the same, and she was still selling a selection of weird, useless ornaments. Hanging outside were brightly coloured buckets and spades, some plastic sand moulds shaped like fishes and stars, and a large blow-up whale. Inside the doorway stood a box of sunhats.

Rose was serving when I entered, so I started to browse. I found small Island-shaped ornaments filled with multi-coloured sands, which I was sure were exactly the same as the one I'd bought my gran when I was about ten. The postcards looked the same too. In the far corner, just as I remembered, were boxes of shortbread and large sticks of rock, but I was pleased to see the sell-by-dates showed they hadn't been lurking around for fifteen years.

I was just thinking that nothing had changed when I noticed a rack of tee-shirts with rude slogans on them. Ah, they were new!

Suddenly Rose gave a squeal and rushed over to me.

'This is so kind of you Jen,' she said, flinging her arms around me.

In between customers, we talked about Mum, my journey, and her future plans.

'I'll take you to see the little apartment I've bought. Of course, it had to overlook the sea and is ideal for locking up and leaving while I go off to Australia to see my cousins,' she said. Then she stopped and looked at me. 'I am doing the right thing, aren't I?'

'Of course you are.'

'It's just that occasionally, when I think about not having the shop, I panic.'

'Just occasionally?' I asked.

'Well, perhaps two or three times an hour,' she admitted.

'You've worked so hard and for so long here,' I said, as I glanced around at the worn displays, the faded carpet, and the chipped paintwork. 'You deserve a break. This place is your past, and it's time to leave it behind and move on.'

Which I suppose was equally true of Alex but, like Rose, every time I thought about a future without him, I started to panic. I'd been working for him for two years and we'd been dating for most of that time. It wasn't anywhere near as long as Rose had been in her shop, but he was a major part of my life.

That evening, Rose took me out to her favourite local cafe for dinner.

'You'll have to make sure you do some sightseeing while you're over here,' she said. 'And a couple of days on the beach would do you good, you're far too pale.'

'I'm here to work, not sunbathe,' I laughed.

'Will Alex be coming over at the weekend?' she asked.

'No. Are you going to have a pud?' If Rose noticed the change of subject, she didn't let on. I knew I couldn't avoid talking about him for long, and I guessed that sooner or later I might just have to talk to him. He'd already left three messages on my mobile saying he needed to see me.

I hadn't expected to, but I slept well that first night. It could have been the salty sea air from my late-night stroll along the beach, or perhaps it was because, with my bedroom window open, I could hear the gentle sounds of the waves breaking over the sand. Whichever it was, it made me so glad I was no longer in the city.

I spent the next morning making large "Sale" banners and draping them across the window. Then I did a turn on the tills, while Rose wrote reduced prices on everything.

'I'm thinking of taking this with me,' Rose said several days later as she held up a hideous two-foot china duck.

I stared at it. 'Wasn't that thing around years ago?' I asked. 'How many did you buy?'

'Two, the other one broke. This one's been lurking here since 1991. No-one's ever wanted him. I thought I'd keep him as a reminder of my very worst stock decision.'

'I bet we can sell him,' I said. I took him from her and slipped a ribbon around his neck and placed him centre stage in the window. I then marked him Bargain of the Day. 'Someone will be daft enough to buy him,' I assured her. But, as I slipped outside to see how he looked, I had my doubts. He really was the ugliest duck I'd ever seen.

But that didn't stop two women arguing over him half an hour later. 'I saw it first,' one shouted clutching the duck tightly. The other woman looked about to start a fight, so I gently took her to the other side of the shop, where I sold her a much better-looking dragon for the same price.

'The duck was nicer,' she said huffily as she left the shop.

'Well, now we know how to get rid of the rubbish,' Rose laughed. Which for some reason made me think of Alex. Had I been so overawed by the fact the boss liked me, that I'd never stopped and really looked at him? Had Alex always been greedy, and I'd just called it ambition because that sounded better?

Rose's hand crept across mine and gave it a gentle squeeze.

'When you want to talk about it, just let me know.'

Her kind words made me crumple and, for a moment, I couldn't stop the tears.

That evening, Rose took me for a drive onto the Downs. We parked and sat looking out over the checkered fields to the town, and then the sea beyond.

'I don't remember the Island being this beautiful,' I sighed.

'You were just a child, Jen. Things looked different back then.' She smiled. 'I can remember you wanted to take home the donkeys from Carisbrooke Castle, yet the snakes at Sandown Zoo scared you so much you cried. And you took one look at our famous Needles and couldn't see what was so special about a few rocks, but then you spent days looking for shells on the beach.' She turned towards me. 'Do you still feel the same today?'

I stopped and thought for a moment.

'Well,' I said, 'Donkeys are lovely, but I've gone off the idea of having one in my living room. Snakes don't bother me now, but I have a feeling I'd get bored looking for shells. Oh, and I was only thinking yesterday that a boat trip out around the Needles would be wonderful. So I guess that does mean I've changed a bit.'

'We all do as we grow older and wiser, which is why changing your mind about Alex isn't necessarily a bad thing.'

'Ah, trouble is I change that at least six times a day,' I confessed.

'He's been round to see your mum,' Rose added. 'It sounds like he's desperate to talk to you.'

'Only because he can't find his way around my filing system.' Which might be unfair, but I was happy hiding on the Island, I didn't want reality phoning me up. But then, I didn't want Alex bothering mum either, so as soon as we got back to the shop, I grabbed my mobile and walked across the road to the beach. It was getting near dusk, so it wasn't hard to find a quiet spot. Alex answered on the second ring.

I had no idea how the conversation would go, but I had rather expected him to start with an apology. Instead, I got a rant about how bad it looked having the boss answer his own office phone. And when I made it clear I wasn't going to catch the next ferry home, he shouted some more.

'You'll regret this when I'm rich. Just remember Jen, I offered you the chance to be a part of all this.'

With that, a wave lapped over my bare foot. It was cool and refreshing, and I knew this simple feeling offered me so much more than Alex ever could.

'I'm sorry it didn't work out,' I said. 'But it's best we find out now. Will you let your family know the wedding is off?'

'What makes you think I'm cancelling it,' he snapped. 'There's plenty of girls who would love to take your place.'

I had to smile. I could just see Alex sitting in the window with Bargain of the Day written across his forehead, and half a dozen women fighting over him.

Perhaps I should have felt sad when I came off the phone, but as I paddled along the water's edge, I just felt free. Then I found an uncomfortable rock to sit on while I phoned my mother.

'She was in floods of tears,' I told Rose when I got back to the flat. 'She said she was so relieved that I'd finally seen sense. Why didn't she tell me she didn't like Alex?'

'Would it have made a difference?' she asked, as she handed me a mug of tea.

'Probably not, but it would have saved me worrying about cancelling the wedding.'

Rose and I stayed up half the night talking about things. Alex, my lack of employment and my fears for the future, as well as how quickly the stock was clearing, Rose's new home and her fears for the future.

'It'll be a whole new world for both of us,' she said before we went to bed – which I think kept us both awake.

It was hot the next morning, and most people stayed on the beach. The shop was quiet, so Rose went to see her accountant while I set about rearranging what remained of the stock. By the time Rose came back, I'd dismantled the centre display, giving the shop a completely different feel.

'I thought it would give the customers more room to browse around the bargain table,' I said pointing to my latest idea.

'You've a good eye for this,' Rose said. 'Why don't you take it over?'

'Take what over where?' I said looking around.

'Take over the shop. My accountant has always said I'd be better off renting out the place rather than selling it, but I didn't want the hassle.

Of course, if it were let to someone I knew, that would be different.'

I stood there with my mouth open, before finally muttering, 'Are you joking?' Seems she wasn't. She gave me the rest of the day off to go and have a think about it.

I drove around for a while trying to take in the idea. Me run a shop on the Isle of Wight? Could I do that? Yet I had spent the other evening looking through the latest catalogues, dreaming about how I'd stock the shop if I had the chance. I'd also fallen in love with some photos Rose had received from a friend of hers.

'Mark's suggesting he hangs his prints in my shop and we split the profit. He's been abroad for over a year and doesn't know I'm closing,' she'd said. 'It's a shame, because he's a wonderful photographer and people will love his pictures. I wish I could help him.'

So I already had a few ideas for the shop, including the way it would need painting both inside and out, and what flooring would be best. I didn't think it would take a heap of money to brighten up the old place, and it wasn't as if I now needed to use my savings on a wedding. It wasn't as if I'd even ordered a dress or anything.

Was that a sign that deep down I'd always had doubts?

I stopped my car along Ryde seafront, and thought how marvellous it would be living so close to a beach that I could walk along it every day. My stepdad was coming up to retirement age, and I knew Mum was trying to get him to buy a holiday place over here. Perhaps if I had the shop, he'd be persuaded.

I knew very little about running a retail business, but Rose had already said she'd help me out at the beginning. It would mean she didn't have to give up her precious shop completely, just that she'd have none of the responsibilities. I could tell she loved the idea.

The big question was, did I want to live on an Island just twenty-six miles by thirteen. Yet I'd been driving round for a couple of hours, and I still hadn't covered half of it. There were lots of little towns with their shops, but just down the road was always beautiful countryside.

Earlier I'd had the chance to really appreciate how green and lush that countryside looked, when I was stuck behind a tractor as it trundled along at ten miles an hour. But at least I'd had a decent view from the car, and wherever

I was on the Island, I was never more than a few miles away from the sea. No, perhaps the question was more, why would I want to return to the city?

I spent the next couple of days working out figures, and I made sure to include all the expenditure items that I felt Des had left off his budgets. Rose was giving me nine month's rent free, but I had to do the place up. It was a risk, but Rose had agreed if I couldn't make a go of it, she'd go back to Plan A, and with that assurance I said yes. Of course I was scared, but everyone supported me. Even my friends liked the idea of somewhere cheap to stay for their weekend breaks.

So, there I was four months later, hanging the 'Open' sign on my very own business. Gone were the buckets and spades, but I still had some postcards, although these were all locally drawn. I also had a range of locally crafted jewellery, pottery and soft toys. At one end of the shop, I had a few tables and chairs, with a selection of drinks and sticky buns, plus a freezer so I could sell ice creams. But, best of all, the walls were covered with masses of beautifully framed photographs.

Rose had been very insistent that I met up with her friend Mark the moment he arrived back from his travels.

'Someone else might snap him up,' she said. 'And I'd hate you to miss the opportunity.'

Silly me, at the time I'd assumed she'd meant his pictures. But I was now pretty sure she hadn't. Although she still denies it.

I liked Mark from the moment I met him. He wasn't that interested in money, but he was interested in other people. He seemed to get on with everyone, which made him as different from Alex as I could possibly find.

Not that I was ready for another serious relationship just yet. Which was what I told Mark as we'd wandered hand in hand along the cliff edge yesterday.

'That's okay Jen,' he'd said. 'Take your time. I'm not in any hurry.'

Which didn't surprise me, because compared to the frantic city life I was used to, nobody on the Isle of Wight was ever in a rush to do anything.

The Swinging Sixties

Despite saying I didn't want a fuss for my birthday, somehow here I was surrounded by all the family. With glasses of Prosecco in hand they were all watching me intently as I took the envelope from Charlotte, my sixteen-year-old granddaughter.

'This is a joint present from Gramps and me,' she said proudly. 'You're going to love it, Nan.'

I could see Pippa frowning and could tell in an instant that my daughter thought I'd hate the present. I'd always been good at reading expressions, and as far as I could see the room was divided equally between those who thought this was a great idea and those who thought it wasn't.

However, Terry was grinning like mad and, after forty-nine years of marriage, I hoped my husband knew me well enough to know what I'd like and what I wouldn't. My guess was that the envelope contained tickets to something. A show in London would be great, or a weekend in a 5-star hotel would be even better. Although both seemed strange things to be a joint present from my husband and granddaughter.

'Come on, Sue, get a move on,' Terry chivvied me along with a big smile. 'If you don't hurry up and open it, we'll still be here on your next birthday.'

'Yes, come on, Nan. I'm dying to see your face when you see what we've bought,' Charlotte urged with youthful exuberance.

I pasted on what I hoped looked like a genuine smile, and wished everyone would stop staring at me. Then I took a deep breath and ripped open the envelope.

I was right, it was tickets. I slipped them out of the envelope and stared at them for a moment. Then I re-read them, just in case I'd read them wrong.

I hadn't!

I knew my smile was still in place, but it was getting harder to keep there. This was my seventy-fifth birthday for heaven's sake, so why on earth would they buy me tickets to the Isle of Wight Pop Festival?

'It'll be great Nan,' Charlotte said. 'We were really lucky to get them because they sold out fast. It's for all day Saturday and Sunday, and the line-up is brilliant.' She then proceeded to list a whole string of names that meant nothing to me.

'Rod Stewart played there in 2017,' Terry added. 'Unfortunately, he's not coming this year. Still, if it's anything like the last Isle of Wight Pop festival we went to, it's as much about the atmosphere as the music.'

'The last time we went to the Isle of Wight it was 1969 and I was twenty,' I pointed out as politely as I could. Oh yes, the smile was starting to slip.

'We'll be camping overnight in the field next door. How great is that?' Charlotte said excitedly. 'Only it'll be in a tent this time. Gramps said you just slept in a group around an open fire last time. I think that sounds a whole lot more exciting, but Gramps says a tent is a must.'

No, at my age a well-sprung mattress, running hot and cold water and a loo en-suite is a must. Of course I didn't say that. I simply gave Charlotte a big cuddle and thanked her. Then I suggested that Terry open another bottle and refill all the glasses.

'I'm going to cut this gorgeous cake Pippa has made me,' I said brightly, grabbing hold of the big kitchen knife. I won't tell you what thoughts were running through my head as I held it in my hand.

As I'd hoped, everyone started talking amongst themselves and my ridiculous birthday present was momentarily forgotten. Although I had a feeling various people would at some point during this evening bring up the subject. What was I going to say when they asked me how I felt about going to a pop festival at my age?

I'd never had much sympathy for people who whinged about big birthdays. I'd always thought they were just another day in your life, so there was no point in making a fuss. Besides, I'd been far too busy enjoying myself to worry about being fifty or sixty or even seventy.

I've no idea why, but I was really surprised to wake up one morning and find I was truly dreading being seventy-five. For the last few months my body seemed to be telling me that I was getting old. Every aching back muscle, every twinge in the knee screamed out that I was almost past it. No matter how many times I told myself that age was just a number, I found I really didn't want that number to be seventy-five.

Not that I sat at home doing nothing all day. Both Terry and I did volunteer work at our local hospice. Terry had been a chef, so now three times a week he went in and made cakes and scones for them to sell in their lovely café. He also cut their grass, while I did a variety of jobs; sometimes weeding, sometimes delivering meals to the in-patients, sometimes serving in the café, sometimes sitting in reception and answering the phones. We both found it very rewarding work.

But three days a week were enough. Long gone were the times when I could clean our house in the morning, spend the afternoon gardening and then go out in the evening. I just didn't have that sort of energy anymore. There was no denying it, I was getting old. Something the mirror insisted on reminding me every time I looked in it, probably because it knew my memory wasn't that great these days.

The family were tucking into the birthday cake when Pippa collared me.

'I'm sorry Mum,' she said. 'I did try to talk Dad out of the festival tickets, but he insisted you'd love it because it was at the 1969 pop concert he'd asked you to marry him. Charlotte got in on the act because she really wants to come with you.'

I shook my head. No matter how hard I tried, I couldn't imagine me wanting my grandparents to come with us all those years ago. No more than I could imagine they'd have wanted to be there. They'd have been completely out of place. Just as Terry and I would be now.

'Why would Charlotte want to go to such a thing with a couple of old fogies like us?' I asked Pippa.

'I have no idea, but then I find teenagers hard to fathom these days.'

I had to smile. It felt like only yesterday I'd been saying the same thing about Pippa, and I had no doubts that my own mother said it about me too when I was growing up.

I couldn't help wondering what had happened to that girl I'd once been. The one who'd marched down the streets of London with flowers in her hair and demanded they ban the bomb. We'd all thought we could change the world. Having listened to the news that morning, I knew we'd failed. But back then it was all "Make Love not War."

Not that I did make love you understand. It might have been the 'swinging sixties' in the heart of London, but in my little town a Saturday evening dancing to The Beatles, then being walked home by a boy who was too shy to kiss me goodnight, was as exciting as it got.

It was a friend at work who'd first suggested a group of us travel down to the Isle of Wight Pop Festival. It was 1969 and I'd been so excited at the thought of seeing the likes of Bob Dylan and The Who. I remember I wore a long skirt and shoved a few undies and some tee shirts

The Swinging Sixties

in a bag and off we went. Oh, those were the days.

I'd been going out with Terry for just over a year, and he'd happily driven a load of us down to Portsmouth. It was amazing how many people he could pack in that old Austin of his. Wouldn't be allowed these days. We'd caught the boat across to the Island, and then we'd just followed the crowds to the site. And what a crowd it was, about 150,000 attended, more than the total population of the Island at the time. We were all squeezed into fields at Wootton, and it was an awesome sight. Terry was correct about something, the atmosphere had been fantastic.

He proposed to me while we were walking around the site early on the Sunday morning. We'd been playing with a huge amount of something called Crazy Foam that someone had brought in for us fans, and I was still giggling when he'd gone down on one knee, taken my hand, kissed it and told me how much he loved me.

'I want to spend the rest of my life with you Sue,' he said.

I'd been so shocked that I'd not known what to say but, darling man that he was, he didn't demand an instant reply. It was much later while Bob Dylan was singing, that I'd cuddled up closer to him and whispered that my answer was yes.

Nobody around us cared that we'd spent the next ten minutes kissing. Everyone was there for a good time, and mostly we all behaved ourselves. I can remember we left our belongings all over the place, and they were still there when we returned. Was that likely to be the case today?

Which made me start to worry about this stupid idea of Terry's. Did he really think this festival would be anything like the '69 one? Back then I was happy to stay up all night. Now I was likely to drop off in the chair about nine-thirty. Also, crowds tended to frighten me these days, especially crowds of youths who would probably be drunk and resentful of people our age gate-crashing their event.

During the rest of the evening, I was teased about being an old hippy and had lots of offers of earplugs, as most of my family thought I'd hate the music they'd be playing. I tried to take it in good spirits, but it didn't help the way I felt

The Swinging Sixties

about the festival, or about me being seventy-five.

When the party finally broke-up and we all said goodbye, I could tell the family thought I'd had the most wonderful birthday, and it was certainly what I told them. But inside I ached. I didn't really want to go back to being that young girl who'd sung "Nights in White Satin," along with the Moody Blues in a field back in the sixties, but I didn't want to be me at my age either.

I had no idea what I wanted. Well, apart from more energy and less aches. I did however know what I *didn't* want, and that was to go to some awful modern pop festival with a load of kids and sleep in a tent. And as soon as I could, I'd tell my stupid husband just that.

Only I didn't do it that evening because Terry was so happy, and I didn't want to upset him. And I didn't tell him the next day because we had friends over. The day after that Charlotte called in to see us and was so excited about our trip that I couldn't say anything then either. I did talk to Pippa the following weekend.

'I was wondering if Charlotte would be happier going to the festival with friends of her own age,' I said, as casually as I could over tea and biscuits.

Pippa banged her mug down very hard.

'I'm not letting Charlotte go to something like this unsupervised,' she said. Which rather mucked up my plans, because there was no way I'd let Charlotte down. If my granddaughter couldn't go without us, then we'd have to take her.

I listened as Pippa laid down the law about how I was to keep a close eye on Charlotte and not let her wander off on her own.

'I seem to remember you demanded, and got, rather more freedom at sixteen,' I pointed out.

'It's a different world today Mum, and I'm relying on you to look after her.'

I did wonder if Pippa would like to take Charlotte in my place, but she soon put me right on that one.

'Sorry Mum,' she said. 'Grant's playing cricket that weekend, and I'm down to do the teas.'

To me she didn't sound at all sorry. You'd have thought she'd have had a little more consideration for her poor old mum. I was seventy-five after all.

Rather disgruntled, I left Pippa's and went home. Without upsetting Charlotte and Terry, I couldn't see any way out of this.

As usual, when you're dreading something, the festival weekend came around far too quickly. Charlotte was beside herself with excitement and even Terry was still full of enthusiasm. Anyone would think he was about to rediscover his lost youth on that tiny little Island.

He seemed a little quiet on the early morning trip to Portsmouth, but maybe that was because Charlotte was so hyped-up she didn't stop talking. The car ferry was very busy, but the crowds were in good spirits.

I had done some homework on the subject, and already knew that the Isle of Wight Pop Festivals had been revived in 2002 and were very popular. Although much smaller numbers went to them than back in the 60's. Now they were in the centre of the Island, but apart from that I wasn't sure what to expect.

The ferry was bigger than I remembered but wasn't as packed as in the 60s, probably down to health and safety. I did, however, think I recognised the road as we drove onto the Island. It was all very well organised, and it didn't take us long to arrive, park the car and find our tent.

And a very posh tent it was too. I didn't ask how much it had all cost, but I was delighted to see that it was near to some very decent loos and some hot showers. There was even some sort of Pamper Parlour. I couldn't help wishing Terry had told me all this in advance as it would have stopped me worrying so much. Knowing I had a decent loo close by helped me relax a bit, as did seeing just how many older folks were around.

'See, I told you there would be others here your age,' Charlotte said, as she slipped her arm through mine.

Walking around the site, there were many more people near her age than mine, but there did seem to be people of all ages, and we certainly weren't the only baby-boomers here. Probably they were all trying to recapture their misspent youths.

The stage was way bigger and more sophisticated than '69, and if you didn't like the music on the main stage, there were lots of smaller tents with different music. There were also fair rides that somehow Charlotte managed to get us to join her on. The big wheel was amazing.

We got talking to another couple of oldies who had their children and grandchildren with them.

'We've come for the last three years,' they said. 'There's something here for everyone.'

We stayed with them when the music started on the main stage, and I found that, far from wanting to run away, I was really loving the bands. The atmosphere was electric, and it was easy to be caught up in the magic of the moment. Not all the music was to my taste, but then it hadn't been back at the '69 festival either.

'Shall we go and grab a drink?' Terry asked after a few hours of watching acts. Charlotte was happy chatting to the two grandchildren who were close to her age so, despite what her mother said, we left them sitting on the grass while we went off and explored some more of the different stalls around the place. Charlotte had a mobile phone, as did we, so finding each other again was easy.

I think it was as we were walking around hand-in-hand that I suddenly realised Terry had been right. This had been the perfect birthday present for me, I was thoroughly enjoying myself.

And the evening was even better. As the stage lights flashed a rainbow of colours into the darkening skies, I found myself surrounded by smiling people all swaying to the beat of the wonderful music. It was a huge crowd, but I didn't feel at all worried. Terry had an arm around my waist, and Charlotte was standing next to me singing her heart out. It was well past my normal bedtime, but I didn't feel in the least bit tired. I didn't feel in the least bit old either, I just felt like me. The person I'd always been before all those silly concerns had started about being "past it."

It was very late when we finally made our way back to our tent.

'Just think of the fun we'd have had if we'd had this set up last time,' Terry whispered, as we snuggled down together.

'I'll have you know I was a good girl back then. If you'd tried any hanky-panky, I'd have socked you one,' I laughed.

'I sometimes wonder if the swinging sixties are just a figment of people's imaginations,'

The Swinging Sixties

Terry said, as he pulled me closer. 'Apart from the great music, all I remember from those days are working long hours and never having enough money.'

'It was more fun in the seventies,' I said. 'After we were married.'

'And the fun isn't over yet,' he promised, before kissing me.

'For goodness sake, will you two settle down and go to sleep. I'm really tired,' Charlotte moaned from her side of the tent.

That's the trouble with the young today, no stamina. We baby boomers can certainly teach them a thing or two. We've always known how to have a good time!

Leeway, Dead Reckoning and Estimated Position

'Your homework is to read the next chapter and practise with the charts before next week,' Josh said, before dismissing everyone in the class except Holly. He turned to her and smiled. 'Do you want to stay behind, love? I can go over those tidal streams again as you don't seem to quite understand them.'

Holly wasn't sure that being the dumbest person in the class was quite the way she'd hoped to attract Josh's attention. But as it was working, she wouldn't complain.

Once the other students had left, Josh came and sat beside her – much closer than was necessary. Which was very nice, but also rather distracting. Holly found it hard enough following what he said normally, this close she had no hope. And it wasn't just his gorgeous blue eyes and cute dimple causing her problems, although they didn't help. It was that she couldn't see the point in learning all this Day Skipper stuff.

Holly hadn't been sailing since she was ten. Back then, her grandfather had informed her that everyone who lived on the Isle of Wight had to try sailing at least once. It was a few years before she discovered that was just his opinion and not a peculiar law for Islanders. She went on to try it four times, before deciding that horse riding was more fun. So why was she doing this evening course? Well, it was all the fault of her sister.

'You'll never get over Sean by staying home moping,' she'd warned Holly a year ago. 'Guys don't come knocking on your door when you're thirty, you have to go out and look for them. I still think on-line dating is the way to go, but as you refuse to do that, why don't you try evening classes?'

A work colleague had lost a lot of money to a guy she'd met on-line, which had made Holly very suspicious of such things. But the idea of going out in the evenings and meeting people, now that did appeal. So she had looked around and decided to join a Spanish for Beginners course.

In the past she'd tried learning it on her phone, but hadn't the incentive to keep it going. She'd hoped this would kill two birds with one stone, as they say. She'd learn another language and get to meet a nice fella.

Only when she started the course, she soon discovered she was the only person under sixty. Four of them were planning on retiring to Spain so were taking it very seriously, but the rest were there to fill their time. Overall, the lessons were fun and the people nice. Okay, she didn't find the man of her dreams, but that didn't stop her enjoying her Thursday evenings.

With other empty evenings to fill, she also joined a photography class. There she met Greg. He was tall, slim, dark and devastatingly handsome. They'd got on great from the start and, eager to show off the gourmet talents he'd learnt on a different course, he'd invited her over to his place for a meal. Of course, he'd already told her all about his partner Ben.

Their cooking and company were very enjoyable, and she was now a regular guest. So, she was getting out way more, even if it wasn't quite in the way she'd hoped.

Leeway, Dead Reckoning and Estimated Position

'Surely there must be better evening classes you can join?' her sister kept insisting. Which was when her brother-in-law had suggested the Day Skipper Theory course.

Holly had thought it was a brilliant idea and loved the thought of being surrounded by all those potential sailors learning their craft. She'd had to wait a few months before there was a new course starting, but there she was, first one on the doorstep when they opened up the classroom a month ago.

But instead of hunky thirty-year-olds, all the males on this course were aged twenty-two and under. And whilst she wouldn't have said no to a toy boy, nobody was asking. This just left Josh, the instructor. Not that she minded, seeing as he was around her age and seemed to like her.

Holly was keen to impress him, but she'd never been good at maths. And trying to convert magnetic compass readings to true compass readings after a long, hard day at the office, was more than her poor brain could take. It was all so baffling, not to mention pointless. Still, as she couldn't tell Josh the only reason she was in his class was to find a man, she spent the next half-an-hour huddled up close to him, trying to understand how tidal streams worked.

'Why don't you come an hour earlier next week,' Josh said, as he helped her on with her jacket. 'Then we can have the place to ourselves and go over things before the class starts.'

It would mean getting time off work, but Holly didn't hesitate, especially when Josh gave her hand a squeeze and assured her that he'd do everything he could to make sure she succeeded in gaining her certificate. She may have been tired and hungry, but she left the college feeling happier than she had in months.

As usual, Holly couldn't be bothered to cook, so headed straight for her local fish and chip shop. Luckily the place was empty tonight, so she didn't have to queue.

'How's your evening classes coming along?' Amy asked as she threw a heap of chips in a bag for Holly.

'Bet you're an expert with that digital camera now,' Matt added, as he took the fish from the fryer.

Holly wasn't quite sure how to answer, she hadn't told many people she'd swapped classes, because she didn't want them figuring out this was simply a manhunt. But as these days she was visiting Matt and Amy's shop on a regular basis, she didn't want to lie to them.

'I feel I've learnt all I can about cameras,' Holly muttered, before adding, 'I used to go out on my granddad's boat when I was a kid, and I wanted to relearn the basics before sailing again.' Which wasn't exactly the truth, but there was always a chance she might go. After all, Josh had a boat.

So it seemed did Matt.

'I did the Day Skipper course about five years ago,' he said.

'Really?' Holly replied, not knowing if this was good or bad. The last thing she needed was Matt asking a load of awkward questions.

'What were you working on tonight?'

'Tides,' she replied, before admitting she was still confused about the way they worked. A while later, Holly found herself seated at the corner table still listening to his explanation. She'd munched her way through her fish and chips, had drunk several cups of coffee and now understood the subject much better. Perhaps Josh's blue eyes had been a bigger distraction than she'd realised.

'Matt doesn't need much of an excuse to stop frying fish and talk about boats,' Amy laughed when Holly said she really ought to leave and let Matt get back to work.

'What's your homework for this week?' Matt asked.

'To read the chapter on Leeway, Dead Reckoning and Estimated Position,' she replied miserably. As she didn't even understand the title, what chance did she have with the content?

Not that she needed to read anything to work out her estimated position in Josh's class. It had to be bottom. Which was why when Matt offered to help her, she accepted at once. Hey, perhaps next week at their extra lesson she'd be able to impress Josh… in more ways than one.

The next evening Holly had to work late, so once again ended up getting her dinner from the chip shop. She was surprised when Matt looked pleased to see her.

'You here for another lesson?' he asked.

'No, sausage and chips,' she laughed. 'I figured Amy wouldn't be too happy if you leave her with all the work two evenings running.'

'Too right,' Amy said. 'He's chained to that fryer tonight whether he likes it or not.'

'Slave driver,' Matt laughed, chucking a chip at her. Just for a moment Holly felt a pang of jealousy, when was the last time she'd been that comfortable as a couple? Even after four years together, she'd always felt she had to be on her best behaviour with Sean, especially in front of other people.

Suddenly Holly realised Matt was speaking to her again.

'If you'd like me to talk you through the chapter, we could do it Sunday morning when the shop's closed.'

'I can't take up your time like that,' Holly insisted.

'He was going out on his boat, but the forecast is for storms,' Amy said. 'Go on Holly, keep the man happy, let him talk about his favourite pastime. It'll make up for him not being out on the water.'

With that a gang of giggling teenagers walked in, so Holly accepted the offer and left.

She wasn't sure if it was the one-to-one teaching, or just Matt's enthusiasm that made the subject so much more interesting and understandable, but by the next Thursday, Holly was sure she'd

Leeway, Dead Reckoning and Estimated Position

be able to impress Josh with her newfound knowledge.

She spent a lot of time getting ready. She arrived at five-thirty and was pleased to see Josh already in the classroom. He flashed her one of his brilliant smiles the moment he saw her.

'I'm glad you've come,' he said, taking hold of her hand. 'I'm sure we can make a lot of progress together in the next hour.'

As he led her to the back of the room, she started telling him all she'd learnt, and was disappointed when he didn't appear to care. She had expected him to sit at the back desk, but instead he started to fiddle with some keys. Then he unlocked a cupboard door and switched on a light. 'It's not very big, but it's comfortable,' he promised.

He had to be joking! Stationery cupboards were for teenagers, not thirty-year-old women. But before she could tell him that, his mobile started ringing.

'Of course I've picked up Billy's medicine, but I told you I had to do some paperwork before the lesson,' he snapped.

Leeway, Dead Reckoning and Estimated Position

There was a pause. 'Of course I'll be straight home after the class. And no, I don't care what you cook for dinner.'

He jabbed at the mobile and stuffed it back in his pocket. 'Sorry, the wife can never resist a chance to nag,' he said, before switching back on his charming smile. 'Now Molly, where were we?'

'The name's Holly, and I was talking about my understanding of how leeway works. And it's my opinion your wife is giving you far too much leeway,' she said before storming out of the classroom.

She was so angry with herself. Just because he'd given her the impression he was single, why had she believed him? And had she really given him the impression that she was so desperate, a quickie in a cupboard would make her happy?

Feeling like a complete idiot, Holly decided not to go straight home. She took herself off to the river, where she went for a long walk in the fresh air. That was it, she was through with evening classes. She'd buy a cat to keep her company in her old age.

It was getting dark by the time she made her way home. She'd calmed down and was feeling hungry, so she called in to buy some dinner. She noticed Matt made sure he was the one to serve her.

'How was the class tonight?' he asked.

'A disaster,' she sighed.

'Oh, I'm sorry to hear that,' he said. 'But I've been looking at the forecast and it's going to be perfect sailing weather on Sunday. The boat is at Yarmouth, and I wondered if you'd like to come out with me and see how things work in the real world.'

Holly stared at him.

'And will Amy be coming with us?'

'Good grief no, she hates the water. I was thinking just the two of us,' he said, giving her a shy smile.

Oh wonderful, two married men hitting on her on the same night. What had she done to deserve that? Now she'd lost her evening classes and a convenient place to buy dinner.

'I don't think so Matt. I'm sure Amy would prefer you spent your time off with her.'

Holly hadn't realised Amy was coming up behind her with a stack of dirty plates until she heard her laugh,

'Don't you think I see enough of him during working hours, without wanting to spend Sunday mornings with him as well? Besides, Matt's dying to show you his boat. Just don't forget to wear something old. My brother might think he owns the QE2, but actually it's just an old tub.'

Her brother? Holly turned back towards Matt, who was still standing there smiling hopefully at her. He was Amy's brother? But she'd always thought… she shook her head. Life was very confusing on occasions. To cover up her total misreading of the situation, she quickly agreed to go out on the boat, before escaping back to the sanity of her flat.

By Sunday, she was wondering if she'd made the wrong decision. She was obviously a terrible judge of character. What if Matt was a serial killer? Although, she had to admit that seemed unlikely, as she felt sure she'd have heard if there had been a recent spate of unsolved murders on the Island.

Matt was already on the boat when Holly arrived at Yarmouth Sailing Club, and suddenly she realised she'd never before seen him dressed in anything other than his working white overalls. Wow, he didn't half look sexy in those blue jeans and fleece.

He took her hand as he helped her on board, and Holly tried not to think about how nice it felt. But if Matt liked it, he didn't show it.

'Right, you ready for your lesson Holly?'

An hour later, Holly found she was rather enjoying herself. The sun was warm on her skin, and the sea sparkled as they sailed through the waves. Matt was an excellent teacher, and far better than Josh at explaining things.

She'd just convinced herself that Matt's interest in her was purely nautical, when he stopped playing with the chart and turned towards her. For a moment they gazed into each other eyes, then she noticed his mouth coming closer and closer and…

'I think it's time for a coffee break,' she said, jumping back and almost falling over a coil of rope. Just because she'd found out the fish and chip shop was a family business and Amy was his sister, that didn't mean he didn't have a wife lurking somewhere in the background. Five minutes later, clutching a steaming mug and feeling more under control, Holly mentioned wives.

'I almost got married back in my early twenties, but things went wrong and we called it off,' he said. 'Then I was too busy, what with Dad being ill and me trying to keep his business going. But since Dad passed away and Amy has been able to join me in the shop, I've now got some spare time. I just need someone to share it with me.' He smiled at her, as he reached across and took her hand.

'I've spent a long time waiting for the right girl to walk into my life, but I have a feeling it was worth it.' He glanced at Holly's notebook before adding, 'Now, if I had to give an estimation of my current position, I reckon I'm heading on the right course. What do you think?'

'Well, I haven't studied the chart in that much detail,' Holly replied as she moved closer to him. 'And I still have a lot to learn, but I reckon you might be right.'

And as Matt started to kiss her, Holly also reckoned she wasn't likely to learn much more about the sea today – but then, who cared about sailing when you were flying this high.

Too Young

I'd always thought retirement was something that happened to other people. Which was why I was shocked to find my husband was starting to plan ours. I mean, why would I retire at twenty-eight? And I was only twenty-eight… inside… where it really counted. My wrinkles were only there to mislead folk.

Geoff looked across his toast and marmalade at me.

'It says this bungalow has sea glimpses from the bedroom, but I'd prefer to sit in the lounge and look out over the water. Wouldn't you?'

I tried hard not to panic. I enjoyed working and whilst I did get more tired these days, it didn't mean I felt ready to retire.

'Geoff, don't you think we're still too young for this?'

'Too young,' he laughed. 'You'll be getting your pension in three months, and I've been getting mine for almost a year now. And we always agreed we'd give up the daily slog together.'

'I know, but that was when I thought we'd be… well… old. Ready to put our feet up.'

'Have you gone off the idea of moving by the sea?' he asked, looking worried.

'Of course not,' I replied. There was a big but on the end of that, not that I said it.

'Well, that's all right then, because I really like the look of these new seafront apartments near Sandown.'

My husband didn't understand. He didn't see the twenty-eight-year-old sitting opposite him. He knew my birth certificate age, and in his eyes that meant I should be ready to slow down. Well, I would be, one day. When I was older.

I could remember my mum when she was sixty-five. She'd looked old, acted old and constantly told my girls she couldn't play with them because she was too tired. So, over the years, when Geoff and I talked about our retirement, I'd assumed we'd be like that too. He'd be a little overweight, going bald, have creaking knees and need glasses to read. I'd have

Too Young

grey hair, wear pearls, tweed skirts and sensible shoes.

Only that wasn't the way it was. Geoff still had perfect vision and played tennis twice a week. I had highlights in my shoulder length hair. I wore jeans and t-shirts, and last month I'd bought some very sexy underwear. Did this sound like someone who was about to settle down to a life of sudokus and jam making?

'Do you really want to retire?' I asked tentatively.

Suddenly Geoff looked serious and a little sad.

'The job's not the same since the boss passed the business over to his grandson. Young Nick has taken on a couple of university graduates who seem to speak a different language from me. I don't fit in anymore. I get the feeling Nick would like me gone so he can just have his own type of people around him.'

'Why haven't you told me this before?' I asked, taking hold of his hand.

'It's only the last couple of months that's been really bad. But now that your job is disappearing, it's convinced me that now is the time to go. And we always said we'd retire together, sell this house and move by the sea. It's crazy that we've both lived our whole lives on the Isle of Wight, both love the sea yet never managed to live close to it.'

I almost pointed out that our Island wasn't exactly big, so the sea was never that far away. But Geoff was right, we had always planned to retire together, and I hated the idea that he was unhappy at work. Trouble was, I wasn't.

Of course, I'd been terribly upset when we'd been told the Council were closing the Day Centre. I'd worked there for almost ten years organising activities for the many vulnerable people who needed the facility. And where would they go now? It wasn't right. I did accept that me finding another job might not be instantaneous, but I'd never doubted I'd find one. Possibly one with fewer hours because I wasn't totally fooling myself when it came to my age, but giving up work completely had never entered my head.

After a weekend of discussions, it was agreed that Geoff should go in on Monday morning and hand in his month's notice. I only had another three weeks before I stopped work. I comforted myself with the fact there wasn't anything stopping me finding a part-time job in the future. I reasoned that Geoff might even want to do the same, although from the way he'd cheered up since we'd made the decision, I wasn't holding out a lot of hope for that.

The next three weeks disappeared fast, and suddenly it was the last day at work. I was heartbroken. The centre had officially closed the week before, the last week was just us clearing the building. A few of my younger colleagues had been offered other care related posts with the Council, and Janice who'd been in charge was leaving the Island.

It was only really me, the oldie, who had nothing to look forward to. I handed back my set of keys, then we all went out for a slap-up meal together. I tried to stay positive, but afterwards I cried all the way home.

A week later, Geoff was given a set of gardening tools, and they took away his company car before handing him his P45. He walked home and looked incredibly happy.

'This isn't right,' I said the first Monday morning when the alarm didn't go off. 'I'm too young to be lazy. Maybe I should get a little part-time job, just something to keep my mind active,' I added, just throwing the idea out there.

'Can't you at least have a few weeks rest before you do anything rash,' Geoff said, frowning at me.

It wasn't that I didn't want to spend time with him, and I tried to explain that I was frightened if I slowed down too much, I'd never speed up again, but he didn't understand my fears. In the end, I promised not to do anything until after we'd looked over his much-admired seafront apartments.

Two days later we had an appointment with the estate agent. Off we went in my car, sorry *our* car. Only having the one vehicle was another thing that was going to take some getting used to. Geoff was sitting in the passenger's seat smiling and holding on tightly to the apartment brochure, while I was just holding on to my doubts and worries about the future.

As I hadn't bothered looking at the brochure in any detail, I didn't have any idea what to expect. The last time I'd seen the place it had been a building site. I was surprised at how impressive the outside looked and the inside, if anything, looked even better. The agent showed us around the first of three different sized flats.

'As you can see, they all have fantastic sea views,' she said, as we stood in the dining part of the lounge.

It was easy to imagine us sitting at the table watching the sunlight dance across the waves as we lingered over a leisurely breakfast. Geoff took my hand as we stepped out onto the balcony. We stood there for a moment watching some children running along the beach.

'Our granddaughters will love this,' Geoff said. And of course he was right. It would be a perfect place to retire… when I was old enough.

'The builders will do you a part-exchange on your current house, which makes things easy for you,' the agent informed us as we were looking around the third and smallest of the flats. 'But the apartments are going fast, so you will need to make a quick decision.'

Oh, that wasn't good. I really didn't feel ready to make any decisions.

'The lift in the apartment block will come in handy as we get older,' Geoff said as we left. Ah, so he didn't think he was that old either.

We spent the rest of the day driving around the Island looking at other potential seafront properties, but I had to agree with Geoff, the new flats were the best.

Then we parked up on the Downs and looked out over the checkered fields to the sea beyond. This really was a lovely Island to live on, and I wondered why we hadn't been walking on these Downs since our children were small. Always too busy I guessed.

'Isn't this great,' Geoff said a little later, before suggesting we go to Godshill for a cream tea. We sat out in the sunshine and scoffed scones and cakes, and it was lovely. It just wasn't something I wanted to do every day for the rest of my life.

Much to Geoff's annoyance, I kept finding excuses for putting off making any decisions over the next few days. Then, after another round of cleaning kitchen cupboards and pulling up weeds, Geoff and I got back from a trip to the supermarket to find a message on our answer phone.

Hi, Lin. It's Mike. I hear your Day Centre has closed. I'm in desperate need of help in the shop. I don't suppose you fancy working for me for a couple of days a week, do you? Please give me a ring.'

Geoff did not look happy.

'I didn't ask him for work,' I pointed out, but my heart soared as I returned Mike's call.

'If I only work two days, that will give us five whole days together,' I reasoned later in bed. Geoff just grunted and turned out the light.

The next morning, I called in to see Mike. He owned a large shop on the outskirts of town. It sold mainly locally sourced foods, plus a wide range of health-related products. There was also a small café, and a section outside that sold seeds and plants for DIY healthy eating.

First of all, he took me around the shop, which of course I'd seen many times, then we went out the back to the storeroom.

'I know you've worked with computers, so this won't be a problem,' he said as he showed me his computerised rotation system.

I didn't like to point out that whilst I had used a computer at work, I only knew the one programme we'd been running for the past six years. Then, back in the shop, he demonstrated his all singing, all dancing electronic tills. I had used a till about thirty years before when I worked for a newsagent. The till we had then was probably itself thirty years old. It looked nothing like this monstrosity.

'It helps with stock control and the VAT returns,' he explained. 'It shouldn't take you long to work out what items are vatable.'

Next, he showed me the credit card machine, the phone system and he talked me through how orders were placed via a tablet.

'Because you'll need to help in the cafe on occasions, I'd like you to go on a Food Hygiene Course. And it would help if you had a First Aid Certificate as well.'

It was almost midday by the time he was finished, and my brain was buzzing. I rang Geoff and was so pleased when he said he'd pop along and pick me up.

'Do you fancy a sandwich at the pub down the road,' he asked, as I climbed into the car.

'And a large glass of wine to go with it would be great,' I replied.

Neither of us said anything about my morning, but as we were sitting waiting for the food, Geoff put some leaflets on the table.

'I nipped out this morning and found a place near to the flats that does yoga lessons for beginners. You've been saying for a few years you fancy trying that. I also found there's a local book club that meets monthly, and some local art classes. Plus, there's a place where you can learn to restore old furniture.'

'Do I want to restore old furniture?' I asked with a smile. 'I thought that was more your thing, darling.'

'You know what I mean,' he laughed. 'It's something I've always wanted to do. Oh, and I picked up a leaflet on a local walking group. You've always said you'd love to do more long walks.' He hesitated before adding, 'If the job is only two days, then we should still have time to do a few of these things – even if we don't move to the area. It's not too far to travel, is it.'

I didn't answer instantly, instead I took a sip of my drink.

'So, how did your morning go?' he asked.

The sun and the wine were helping me relax a bit. I took a deep breath.

'I want to go for it,' I told him.

'Oh, well, if you're sure.' He stared miserably into his beer.

'Yes, I think I'd like to go for apartment 10. You know, the one with the two balconies and the larger second bedroom.'

He looked up at me and beamed.

'You want to go ahead with the move? Does that mean you're not going back to work?'

I sighed. The headache was easing.

'It's not that I'm too old to learn about VAT rates or how to work complicated computer systems,' I explained. 'But it does seem a lot of effort just for two days a week.' I picked up some of the leaflets. 'And I reckon between moving home and joining even some of these, we'll have plenty to keep us active.'

'And our daughter says the kids will love spending their holidays by the beach,' he said.

'That's why we'll need the bigger second bedroom.' I knew this was all going to take some adjusting to, but it had to be better than wrestling with that hideous till and its hundreds of buttons.

'Do you want another glass of wine?' Geoff asked.

'Why not,' I murmured. After all, nothing needed my urgent attention this afternoon. I'm retired don't you know.

It's a Crime

My sister gives a disapproving snort.

'Oh, for goodness sake Esme, don't be so ridiculous. You know what your problem is, you spend far too much of your time reading those silly crime novels instead of having a life.'

'I don't have a problem,' I sigh. 'All I said was, it seems odd that a guy would come into the museum a few times on his own and not spend very long looking at the exhibits.'

'He's probably disappointed with what you have to offer,' she replies haughtily before giving a little snigger.

You'd think we were still seven and nine, not twenty-seven and twenty-nine. But I guess if we haven't resolved our differences by now, we probably never will. Cassie has never understood my fascination in our Island's past. The Isle of Wight might be small, but our history is vast.

Dinosaurs roamed here, other countries have invaded us, a king was once imprisoned here, a queen has sought refuge here. We have castles, prisons, and a world-famous sailing regatta. Every town has a tale to tell, and I'm proud of the museum I'm in charge of.

Cassie sees it as me living in the past, and not being part of the real world. She works at the local hospital and sees far more of the "real world" than I could ever stomach. I'm the first to admit that Cassie's job is far more important than my own, but I'm a little fed up with her constantly pointing it out. Luckily, we don't see a lot of each other these days, and we're only together now because it's our mother's birthday. At least Mum likes the museum and comes to all the exhibitions I organise. She's never once been to the hospital to see what Cassie gets up to in the operating theatre. With this satisfying and rather childish thought, I tuck into my slice of birthday cake.

However, I must admit that Cassie does have a point. What is so strange about some guy visiting the museum a few times. Except something doesn't feel right.

The next few days are busy, and I don't give him another thought, but then suddenly I look up and he's back. I recognise him instantly. Maybe it's his dark brown eyes, or that dimple on his chin, or maybe it's the dirty mark on the arm of his raincoat that makes him so memorable. I'm instantly on edge as he pays for his ticket by cash. He's always done that, well cards can be traced, can't they.

'Is there anything that particularly interests you? If so, I can point you in the right direction,' I say, hoping to sound helpful and not like I'm interrogating him. But before he can answer, my stupid phone rings.

He mutters something indecipherable and hurries away.

As soon as I've dealt with the call, I go over to the CCTV monitors as I feel I need to keep an eye on this guy. And watching him proves quite easy to do, seeing as he's taking photos of all my CCTV cameras. He's also making notes. I don't care what my sister says, this is very suspicious behaviour.

The cosy crime novels I read always has a murder or two but, as good as my imagination is, I don't for a moment think this man is planning to kill someone in the museum. Or I hope not, as there is only me. But everyone knows that professional criminals case out properties before robbing them, and that is what he seems to be doing. So, is he planning to rob the museum? But that makes no sense, why would anyone consider robbing this place?

Whilst I loved the museum, I'd be the first to admit there's very little of value on display. Items of historical interest yes, items worth stealing no. That doesn't mean to say some of the travelling exhibitions, that I can sometimes persuade to spend a week or two on our lovely Island, aren't worth stealing. But we don't have anything like that currently in the museum. I glance at the diary and see the next such exhibition is in five weeks. I've had to arranged for the museum's insurance cover to be increased to satisfy the owner, but surely no one is going to spend weeks planning to steal a vintage model railway. Even if this one is very impressive.

I'm looking forward to the railway arriving because I already have a full week of primary school children booked to visit. Showing kids around is the part of my job I love best. We had a teddy bear exhibition six months ago, and the youngsters loved that one. The twenty doll's houses we had here for a whole month last year, was the best attended exhibition I'd organised. However, I normally make our exhibits more applicable to the Isle of Wight. Ones featuring famous people from the past and present who were born locally are always popular, as are old photos of the towns.

We often hold art exhibitions for local painters, but the only one of those coming up is for the woman who regularly hires a room to try and sell her paintings. She's good, but they seldom fetched more than £350 each. Certainly nothing worth planning a robbery around.

I look once more at the monitor, the man has moved into a different room and although I can't see exactly what he's doing, it looks like he might be making a sketch of it. It's the room I've done up to represent a street scene from the 40's, and it goes along with the war memorabilia in the previous room. I spent months making the displays, and local people have been so generous donating relevant items. That room is a favourite with the children too, they love looking at old fashioned tills and weighing machines, but half the things on display in the shop windows are just bits of cardboard I've covered with printed pictures of old packets of soap powder and the like. It simply makes no sense that anyone would be planning to break in here, especially as the local police station is only just down the road. Mind you, it's only open two days a week, so probably not much of a deterrent.

I decide to try to talk to the guy and see if that eases my mind a bit. But as I'm walking out of my office, a family of four arrive. They're holiday makers, and by the time I've taken their entry fee, walked them around the first room and explaining some of the Island's history to them, the guy has left. When looking back over the CCTV footage, I see that he stopped and took some photos of my office and our entrance on the way out.

That evening, I sit in bed reading my latest book. The heroine is currently driving around trying to solve the murder. I know she'll succeed because she always does. But despite reading so many of these crime novels, I have no real idea how to solve a mystery. Usually the heroine knows the victim's name, and almost all the people suspected of killing them. My mystery isn't so easy. For a start there hasn't been a crime, just a suspicious guy aged about 30. And how am I supposed to find out his name?

I think about contacted my boss for advice. I see little of him, as the museum is only a sideline for him, and he largely leaves me to run it. But what can I say that doesn't sound completely crazy? Anyway, I've already downloaded an image of the man from the CCTV recording, and I've written down the dates and times he's visited - just in case! What else can I do?

It's almost a month later when he turns up again. This time quite near to me closing up for the day. Same raincoat with its dirty mark, but this time it's soaking wet. It's been raining hard all day and if he's just looking for shelter, I can think of a dozen places he could go who don't charge an entry fee.

'You can't stay away from the place, can you,' I say, as I take his cash.

'You've noticed,' he replies.

Argh, that was stupid. Will he now need to silence me? But he isn't looking at me in a menacing way, although he does look a little uncomfortable. Well, that makes two of us.

I feel sure he's about to say something else when Charlie, our handyman, choses that moment to walk in. He's got the extra trestle tables I need for the model railway display. I can't do anything but watch as my potential burglar walks towards the first display room. I grab the keys to the room where the model railway is going to be housed and follow Charlie.

'Sorry I'm late,' he says 'I'd have been here lunchtime, but the van had a flat tyre. I've got six more tables in the van. Will that be enough?'

I reassure him that eight is plenty, and we set about putting them up and arranging them in the way that's been requested. It's way past closing time before it's all finished. As Charlie's packing up his toolbox, I begin my normal end of the day routine. I'd assumed the guy would have left by now, so am surprised when I see him lurking by one of the displays. Surprised and a little concerned.

'It's past closing time,' I say sharply.

'Sorry, I didn't notice,' he replies, but he doesn't hurry off. In fact, he moves very slowly towards the entrance, and I have a feeling he's waiting for something. Or maybe someone? Glad that Charlie's still around, I call out to him. The man seems to take the hint and leaves. But I'm now even more convinced he's some sort of criminal. What can I do? The police are busy solving real crimes, will they be interested in my suspicions? Of course not. But I will give the owner a call this evening, and hope he takes me seriously.

After locking up, I get into my car and am trying to pull out of the car park when who should I see drive past but my would-be criminal.

There are three cars between us when we pull up at the traffic lights. I can see he's indicating to turn right. My route home is straight on, but that isn't what any of the heroines in my books would do. They'd use this opportunity to follow him. And if I do that, then at least I might have an address for him. That must be more use than just a grainy photo off the CCTV camera. With a tingling feeling in my stomach, I grip the steering wheel firmly and set about following his car. There's now only one vehicle between us, but that means I can't see his licence plate, but I do make a mental note of the make and colour of his car.

All three cars continue along the road for about five minutes, then he turns off into a small estate on the outskirts of Wootton. Now I'm directly behind him and try to stay well back, because that's what they do on the TV. He turns into a cul-de-sac, so I quickly park my car and get out. Oh yes, I know better than to take my car down a dead-end street.

I grab my phone and take a photo of the road name, then I wait a few minutes before going to look for his car. It's quite a long cul-de-sac, and I've walked quite a way before I spot his car parked on a driveway. With a thumping heart and trembling hands, I hold up my phone to take a photo of both the car and the house. Only I can't see the number plate or the house number from that angle, so I have to move closer. In fact, I have to get right in front of the house before I can get a decent view. I'm just taking the photo when he opens his front door.

Even though I'm on the other side of the road, he sees me instantly, and we just stand there staring at each other for a moment. He looks puzzled. I'm guessing I look terrified. He walks onto the pavement.

'You're the girl from the museum,' he says.

My brain is telling me to run but I've never been a sprinter, and my car isn't close. Without his raincoat on, I can see he looks very fit. He'll easily catch me.

'Did you follow me home?' he says.

Without engaging my brain, I say the only words that come into my head.

'Are you planning to rob my museum?'

He opens his mouth, then closes it again, then he bursts out laughing.

'I'm sorry,' he splutters when he eventually stops. 'I guess I can see why you'd think that. I've wanted to talk to you, but you've always been busy. And not over-friendly,' he adds.

'I'm always friendly,' I state firmly, before realising that I've always viewed him with suspicion, so I probably haven't been very friendly. And with that it starts pouring with rain again.

'Why don't you come inside, and I'll explain everything,' he says.

Inside! Is that sensible?

'My name's Nathan and I'm perfectly harmless, I promise,' he adds. And he does look nice with his sparkling brown eyes and a smile that seems to brighten the wet, miserable day.

None of my fictional heroines would run away at this point, so I take a deep breath and follow him inside, and out of the rain.

Over a coffee, Nathan shows me the four books he's already had published.

'I've seen some of these in the window of the local book shop in Cowes,' I gasp, before admitting I haven't read any. 'I tend to choose books with female lead characters,' I explain.

'Well, in the book I'm currently writing, my very male detective is investigating a robbery and murder in a museum. Whilst the museum is a lot bigger and more upmarket than anything we have on the Island, I've found all sorts of ideas coming to me as I walked around yours.'

'Is that why you photographed the CCTV cameras?'

'I find it useful to be able to see these things when I'm describing them, and it was helpful to see where they were positioned. Yes, I know I can look up things on the internet, but it's not the same as seeing it in real life. I've wanted to talk to you about the security system, but you were always busy…' he trails off.

'And not very approachable. Sorry about that.'

'Well, I now understand seeing as you thought I was a potential thief.' Then he looks at me. 'Out of interest Esme, what did you think I was going to steal?'

Ah, I'd hoped he wasn't going to ask me that. Feeling somewhat silly, I shrug.

'People buy strange things these days.' Then I grin. 'Actually, I couldn't think of a thing you'd want to steal, but that didn't stop my over-active imagination.'

Somehow the coffee stretches into dinner at the pub down the road. I tell Nathan all about my love of books, and he tells me about his love of writing. We never stop talking and I can't remember the last time I've had such an enjoyable evening.

I discover that Nathan is single, which doesn't surprise me what with him going around in a dirty raincoat.

'I've never noticed the mark,' he admits as he walks me back to my car.

We stand by it and chat for a while longer.

'You know, if this was a romantic novel, I reckon about now I'd have the couple staring into each other's eyes and possibly kissing,' he says with a smile.

I'm not sure how to respond.

'I used to read romance,' I say. 'But I gave it up because it's all happy-ever-after and life isn't like that.'

'Whereas finding dead bodies around every corner is far more realistic?' he laughs.

'Good point, and maybe the truth is that reading romances just makes me feel lonely,' I confess.

Whereupon Nathan leans forward and kisses me. And a very lovely kiss it is too. Happy ever after? Who knows? But I have a feeling that if I'm not careful, this would-be thief might just steal my heart.

Unrealistic Expectations

'What about putting it in the main bedroom, right opposite the twin beds? That way he's bound to see it,' Kim, my sister, suggests as we look for somewhere to hang my painting of Andrew's yacht.

'But I can't be sure that's the room he'll sleep in,' I reply. 'He's the main man after all, he might go for the smaller bedroom, so he doesn't have to share.'

'Hmm, that's a good point,' Kim agrees. 'How about hanging it at the bottom of the stairs, then everyone will see it as they are coming down?'

'I did think about that, but all the crew will have bulky sailing bags, and the hallway isn't very wide. I'm afraid the painting might get damaged if we put it there.'

Which only leaves the lounge.

'Well, Ellie,' Kim says, 'You'll just have to hope they spend some time in the living room and aren't out partying every night. Of course, you could always do the sensible thing and simply tell the man you've done a painting of his yacht, then ask if he'd like to see it. After all, if you're going to try and earn a living from your art, you're going to have to man-up and learn to promote yourself.'

I look at my sister. Kim's so different from me, she's always been full of confidence, even if it is sometimes misplaced. All my life it seems she's been telling me to man-up and maybe she's right. If I'm going to try and make a career out of painting I'm going to have to step outside my comfort zone.

'I still think your expectations are unrealistic. This Andrew fella isn't the answer to all your prayers you know,' Kim continues. 'It's a year since you've seen him. Do you really expect him to come in and solve all your problems? I mean, what do you really know about him?'

Oh no, not this again.

Unrealistic Expectations

'I don't have any expectations regarding Andrew,' I point out for about the fiftieth time. 'I'd love it if he liked my painting of his boat, especially if he liked it enough to buy it. And I'd be over the moon if he could recommend me to his wealthy yacht owning friends, but I'm realistic enough to know it's a long shot. It's just one I think is worth taking.'

'It's not him buying the painting that concerns me, as you well know. It's the fact you've put your life on hold for the past year waiting for him to return.'

I shake my head, what's the point in arguing with her. Kim is convinced that I've not been out on a date for the past twelve months because of Andrew. Just because I happened to mention last Cowes Week that Andrew was tall, blonde and devastatingly handsome and, that with a little encouragement, I could fall madly in love with him, didn't mean I *had* fallen madly in love with him.

Of course I'd fancied him, what red-blooded twenty-eight-year-old wouldn't? And, if I'm totally honest here, there have been nights in my lonely bed that I have thought about him, but that doesn't mean I've turned down dates because of him.

What my sister fails to take into consideration is the fact I work all hours doing other people's accounts to pay my bills. The rest of my time I'm in my studio painting in the hopes of one day giving up said accounts.

I haven't been out on a date because I haven't been anywhere to meet anyone to ask me. Besides if they did, I'm not sure I'd have the time to go. I have tried to explain this to Kim, but she won't listen.

'Are you going to help me hang this picture or not?' I ask her. 'I've told them the house will be ready any time from two.'

After she's gone, I look at the painting. I reckon it's my best work to date, but then I have put a lot of time and effort into it. I've been concentrating on seascapes for the past two years, and in particular pictures of boats on The Solent. That's one of the benefits of living on the Isle of Wight, there's always plenty of sea and boats around for inspiration.

My family and friends tell me I'm good, but there's always this nagging doubt that I'm rubbish and they're just being kind. What if

Andrew doesn't recognise his own boat in the picture? What if he doesn't even notice the painting? Worst of all, what if he tells me he hates it?

There's something special about living in Cowes during this famous sailing regatta. Each year hundreds of boats, sailors and spectators invade our little corner of the Isle of Wight. People of all nationalities come here for the sailing and partying, and with all these visitors, accommodation is at a premium.

Which is why the Airbnb market does well in the summer on the Island. A few years ago, a friend started letting out her home during the summer to increase her income, and it gave me ideas. If I wanted to paint all year round, I needed a decent studio that let in the light. The income from my accounts work paid my bills, but renting out the house during the summer would pay for a loan to build a proper studio in the garden.

Well, it's slightly more than a studio, it's also got a shower room, a corner with a sink, microwave and small fridge, and enough space to put a blow-up bed. My sister's good enough to let me leave my excess clothes at her place, and to let me use her washing machine for the summer. So, as much as Kim nags and annoys me on occasions, she really isn't a bad sister. Without her help I'd never have the studio. Which luckily I only have to live in for a few months a year.

I've had two couples stay so far this summer, but it's Andrew's visit I'm obsessing over. He's texted me several times over the past few months, and each time he's said he's looking forward to seeing me again.

As I await his arrival, I'm getting more and more nervous. I keep telling myself it's just the painting, but I can't help remembering the kiss he gave me just before he left last year. The kiss I've never mentioned to Kim. The kiss I'm sure meant absolutely nothing to him. The kiss I keep telling myself meant nothing to me either.

I check the house and the painting far too many times, and on this hot and sticky August day I find I can't concentrate on anything as the hours tick by. It's not until six, just as a cooler breeze arrives, that Andrew turns up. He's as handsome as I remember, and I feel quite lightheaded as he smiles at me. Which I put down to not having eaten much today.

'Ellie, it's wonderful to see you again,' he says, giving me a quick peck on the cheek.

Perhaps not quite the reunion of my dreams, but acceptable. I want to say something witty and memorable at this point, but all I can manage is, 'Here are the keys. If you have any problems, I'm out the back the same as last year.'

'That's handy,' he says with a wink, before disappearing into my home.

Last Cowes Week, when I first met the guys staying at the cottage, it didn't take long for me to work out Andrew was in charge. I found out he was the owner of a rather impressive fifty-five-foot yacht, and he told me he spent most of the year racing it in various locations around the world. Which I figured was a nice lifestyle, if you could afford it.

I could hardly believe it when, towards the end of the week, he'd invited me to one of the many posh cocktail parties. Of course, I knew they took place around Cowes during this week, but I'd never been to one. An evening in the beer tent was much more my style. However, a chance to see what one of the posh parties was like wasn't something to be turned down. I guessed

I'd be the only female in the place not flaunting a designer label, but so be it.

I did have a sexy little black dress and even if my outfit was second-rate compared to the other women's, my companion wasn't. I felt a million dollars dancing with Andrew. He moved beautifully. He was sophisticated but witty and, given the chance, I could have fallen in love with him there and then. But I wasn't given the chance because it was only one dance, and we only stayed at the party forty-five minutes.

Even Cinderella's prince danced with her for longer and, from what I remember, Prince Charming didn't move on to another party and leave her to walk home alone. Still, it was probably a once in a lifetime chance to see how the other half lived, so I didn't regret going.

Two days later Cowes Week was over, and Andrew popped round to my studio to return my house keys. I can't remember exactly what he said, but he asked me if it was possible to rebook the cottage for the following year, and when I said yes, he kissed me. Ah, the kiss, now I remember that very well.

Unrealistic Expectations

How quickly the year has flown by. Now here he is back in my house. Will he notice the painting? Oh god, what if he thinks I'm a lousy artist? I go and make myself a coffee and try not to think about it. Some hopes.

During the night I find myself asking the question - if I had to choose between Andrew loving the painting or loving me, which would it be? Maybe Kim was right, maybe my expectations of this week really were far too unrealistic.

After a largely sleepless night, I hear Andrew and his crew leave the house early. I'm disappointed he hasn't been in to see me, but I have plenty of work to do. Only it's hard to settle, so I walk down to The Parade hoping to catch a glimpse of his boat out on the water. Trouble is, the Solent's just a mass of white sails and colourful spinnakers, it's like looking for the proverbial needle in a haystack. So, I set about wandering around the newly erected tents instead.

There's some live music, and it's hard not to get caught up in the atmosphere as I wander through the crowds. Eventually I decide I must do some work, so make my way back to the studio.

After three more days of waiting for a knock on my studio door, I decide enough is enough and I need to get out of this cramped room. So I arrange to meet with a group of friends in the pub for the evening.

I've just locked up and am halfway down the side path when Andrew appears.

'Hi Ellie, I've been trying to get in to see you, but things have been so hectic,' he says flashing me one of his brilliant smiles. 'Are you rushing out, or can you spare me a minute?'

I glance at my watch. Not that there's any doubt I'll give him all the time he needs, especially when he adds, 'I'd like to talk to you about your painting of my boat.'

It's strange going into your own home as a guest, but soon we're standing in my lounge staring at the picture of his yacht.

'I remember you said you painted, but you didn't say you were this good. It's fantastic, Ellie. How did you do it?'

'I bought copies of the professional photos taken last year. I just isolated yours from the rest and placed it in the Solent on its own. I'm glad you like it,' I say, which must be the understatement of the year.

For months I've been rehearsing my sales pitch, but now Andrew's standing so close my mind goes blank. Luckily, I don't need to say anything because he turns to me and says, 'I don't suppose it's for sale is it.'

'It most certainly is. And I'd love to paint other boats, if I can get some commissions,' I say in a rush before I lose my nerve.

'Perhaps I can help with that.'

How I stop myself throwing my arms around him, I don't know. But I can't keep the grin from my face as we walk to the Yacht Haven discussing prices. Kim had told me to start high and negotiate, but instead I ask him what he thinks it's worth. Which turns out to be very sensible, because I would never have asked that much.

As Andrew buys a round of drinks, I text my friends to say I'll be late. During the next hour, he introduces me to three of his friends and shows them photos of my painting. Two of them are interested in seeing the real thing with a view to me painting their yachts. Talk about a dream evening. Andrew even walks me to the pub where I'm meeting my friends, and he promises to speak to several more of his yacht owning mates over the next few days. What a star, I almost float into the pub.

The next morning, I awake to find that summer has disappeared, and it's now wet and windy. Not that I care about mundane things like the weather, I'm too busy setting out my best paintings for the guys who are coming back with Andrew after the racing.

'Oh Kim, you're never going to believe this,' I say that evening. 'I have one definite commission, and two possibles.'

'That's fantastic Ellie. Perhaps this bloke isn't as bad as I'd feared.'

I grin.

'Ah, I see something else has happened. Come on, tell me everything.'

'It's nothing much,' I assure her. 'He's just asked me out on his boat tomorrow. Seems two of his crew are going back to the mainland tonight, and with this wind he needs to make up the numbers.'

'But you've only been sailing a few times.'

'I told him that, but it's only to sit on the side.'

'You mean he wants you as extra ballast? How romantic!' she laughs.

I don't admit it to Kim, but I have the feeling Andrew has asked me purely out of desperation. However, I'll settle for that.

The next day, I'm up extra early. The weather is still bad, but I'm too excited to worry about it. I just wish I didn't have to wear the waterproofs I've borrowed. They make me look like a fat Santa. Still, I'm sure Andrew won't hold it against me.

At eight-thirty, I walk down to the boat with Andrew and his housemates. There I see the rest of the crew.

'How many of us are there?' I ask, looking at the mass of bodies running around.

'Hopefully eleven,' Andrew says, before calling out, 'Anyone seen that guy who promised to join us?'

'Noah arrived ages ago. I've sent him off to buy some supplies. He should be back any minute,' one of the crew says.

It's a lot windier out on the water than I'd anticipated, and there's nothing friendly looking about those waves. I hope I won't disgrace myself by being seasick. As I have nothing else to do, I help Noah when he gets back. We start chatting as we unpack the bottled water and baguettes, and he tells me he works on the ferries and only has today off to go sailing.

'I'm lucky to find a place on a boat, especially one like this,' he says, looking at the fancy electronics. 'This lot must have cost a fortune. Last year I was on a boat built in the 1930's that was mainly held together with tape. However, we all had a lot of laughs sailing it.'

That's the nice thing about Cowes Week, anyone can enter. Long gone are the days when it was purely the sport of the rich. Not that there isn't the odd millionaire or three milling around.

The next hour is hectic. As we set off for the start line, Andrew begins calling his instructions over the noise of the wind. Any ideas I have about this being a pleasant day on the water disappear as I'm told off twice for not moving fast enough. Andrew's out to win, and I realise if I want to impress him, I'll have to take this seriously.

I've never been in a race before and whilst it's exciting, it's also exhausting. Andrew's a hard taskmaster and never stops screaming at everyone. Thankfully, as Noah and I are only here to add weight, he doesn't yell at us too much. The conditions are rough, which mean Noah and I keep getting drenched, but we sit and talk and joke together which helps make the experience a little more pleasant.

Heading towards the end of the race is stressful, and all I feel is relief when we finally cross the finish line. As we are in first place, I expect Andrew to congratulate his crew, but all he does is harangue everyone for the fact that it was such a close call at the end.

'I wouldn't want to sail regularly with someone like that,' Noah comments.

Something I agree with whole heartedly. Fun it wasn't.

Packing up the boat is a long job, and Noah and I help as much as we can. We're collecting the rubbish from below deck when Noah suggests we go for something to eat when we get off the boat. I'm just about to say I'd love to, when we hear Andrew being asked if he wants to invite the two "extras" to the beer tent to celebrate the win.

Noah and I look at each other as we strain to listen to Andrew's reply.

'I wasn't going to bother inviting what's-his-name, but I thought I'd ask Ellie. Her house might be poky, but it's very convenient, so I need to keep her sweet.'

Well, that tells me, doesn't it. Any dreams of Prince Charming sweeping me off my feet die instantly. Mind you, having spent a large part of the day listening to him yelling at people, I can't say I'm going to lose any sleep over him.

'I've never liked stuck-up grotty yachties,' Noah states as he takes the black sack of rubbish from me.

'No, neither have I,' I respond. Although I had thought Andrew was better than that.

'Do you think he's buying my painting just so I'll rent him my cottage next year?' I add, as all my insecurities bubble to the surface again.

'Didn't you say he'd recommended you to his friends?'

I nod.

'Well, he wouldn't do that just to keep you sweet. He must admire your work.'

Which is lovely of Noah to say and does make me feel a little better.

Noah and I go up on deck and are about to get off the boat when Andrew calls me over.

'Don't go far,' I tell Noah.

Taking a deep breath, I walk towards Andrew.

'Will you join us for a drink?' he asks. 'Just you Ellie, not that other guy.' He makes it sound like I'm someone special, and I suddenly have the urge to hit him.

'I'm going for a drink with Noah, but don't worry I'll still rent the house to you next year.'

I can tell from Andrew's expression that he's realised we overheard him. And, despite what Noah said, I need to know.

'Why are you buying my painting?'

'That has nothing to do with your house. I'm buying it because it's damned good and, I can assure you, that's the only reason I'm recommending you to my friends.'

I can tell he means it.

'That's all right then.' I say, smiling again. 'I just needed to be sure.'

'Ellie, please come for a drink with me.'

Unrealistic Expectations

I shake my head. 'But I might charge you more rent next year to make up for missing out on the beer.'

'That seems fair enough,' he laughs.

Andrew holds my hand as he helps me off his boat and, just for a moment, he looks as if he's thinking that perhaps I am someone he should get to know better. Which is nice, but I know a business-type relationship is all I want. I could never be comfortable in Andrew's cocktail party, designer clothes world.

'Everything okay?' Noah asks as I join him by the rubbish bins.

'Everything's fine.'

'Good,' he says. 'So do you fancy some fish and chips?'

Now that is something I feel very comfortable with, especially when Noah takes my hand as we start walking.

Funny, but this Cowes Week is turning out much better than I'd ever expected.

Letting Go

Our house is packed with family and friends. I'm standing close to Lisa, my wife, trying to support her as we're made to listen to yet another relative twittering on.

'Oh my dear,' she says, clasping Lisa's hand tightly. 'You're being so brave.'

I watch as Lisa swallows back her tears. She looks terrible. Over in the corner, I can hear my mother sobbing noisily.

'I think you should have bought way less sausage rolls and far more tissues,' I whisper, attempting to lighten the mood. The glare I receive makes me wish I hadn't bothered.

It's not that I'm heartless. Really, I'm not. It's just that I don't see why everyone is getting so upset. Isn't this supposed to be a celebration?

'I still think the girls are being a little selfish wanting to all leave home on the same day,' I hear Lisa's best friend whispering loudly to another so-called friend.

Letting Go

I give up! Why is everyone so determined to make matters worse? Why shouldn't our daughters leave home together? After all, eighteen or so years ago they arrived together. And did people weep and wail then? No, everyone just congratulated us.

'Oh, triplets,' they cooed in silly voices. 'Aren't they adorable. You're so lucky.'

Well sorry, at the time I didn't feel very lucky. Of course, we knew there were going to be three babies. Lisa was a twin herself, and there were twins on my side of the family, so we'd already discussed the possibility of two babies before the first scan.

We'd said we only wanted two children, and Lisa had reckoned it would be nice to only have to go through it all once. I hadn't been totally convinced, I was twenty-seven and more than a little apprehensive at the prospect of one child. Two of them screaming to be fed at the same time was actually quite scary.

Oddly enough, come the day of the scan, as I was watching the screen, I wasn't even thinking about twins. I was just praying everything would be fine. The nurse gave a little yelp and pointed to two tiny heads. Lisa started smiling and I took hold of her hand. Then, before I could process this information, and like some supermarket special offer of buy two and get one free, the nurse gave another yelp and proclaimed it was triplets.

Even Lisa had look shocked at that news. But once we'd been reassured that all the babies were looking good, she bounced back.

'Oh Mike, I can't wait to tell our folks,' she'd said excitedly. 'Isn't it great that you didn't get that job in Bristol last year, at least by staying on the Island we've got plenty of family around to help us.'

I have no idea what I said to that. I think I was in what is known as "A State of Shock."

Not getting the job in Bristol the year before had been a big disappointment. It would have been a step up the ladder with a very nice pay rise. I'd been born here on the Isle of Wight, but I'd loved my three years away at Uni. When I graduated, I came back to my parent's house in Cowes and started applying for jobs on the mainland. Getting a foot in the door of a competitive marketplace proved harder than I'd anticipated, so I ended up taking a position locally.

Letting Go

Despite filling in hundreds of application forms, I never found the prefect job, but one day I just happened to find the prefect lady. I met Lisa and fell in love. Suddenly staying on the Island wasn't such a hardship, although I'd always kept an eye on available jobs the other side of the Solent. Or I had been right up until that moment when there were three tiny heads on that screen.

I don't remember much about the next few months except that I fussed a lot over Lisa. Lisa's mother and sister fussed over her and my mother fussed over her. In fact, it seemed like half the world was fussing over my wife. No one fussed over me, but my mates did suggest that I should go to as many football matches as possible, as I'd never get to see another one once the babies arrived.

Not that I did have time for football, even before they popped out. Both our parents kindly got together and helped us buy a bigger house, so with moving and decorating, not to mention working and getting a much bigger garden under control, I had little time to consider the future. Or maybe I was just burying my head in the sand.

Letting Go

I've since been told that most new fathers think they know how life will be when the baby arrives - and that most of them are wrong. But I'm not sure I even tried to picture what life would be like with three babies. It was simply too much to get my head around.

'Oh Mr Gray, aren't they all adorable,' they said at the hospital as number three made her appearance into the world.

I remember looking at three tiny, helpless babies and suddenly I wasn't scared anymore. Now it was full blown panic!

How would we cope? Could I earn enough? How do you change three nappies at once? Of course, no one noticed how scared I was. I felt so guilty because everyone seemed so pleased, while I just felt terrified. Naturally, I was far too manly to admit it, and the panic did subside. It only took about five years!

I look across the room at my beautiful daughters. They're so grown-up and confident, and I'm very proud of them. Natasha's off to university, Katie's about to start an apprenticeship with a hotel chain in London, and Beth's off to Australia for a year.

Letting Go

Katie managed to get access to her room in the staff quarters of the hotel at the end of last week, so at the weekend she took her car to London filled with Beth's large suitcases, and most of her own things. It means that tomorrow they'll have room in the car for their last bits, plus all of Natasha's uni gear. I'm still not sure how they've managed to organise their departure together, but they've always done as much as possible as a threesome, so why not this?

So much has changed in the last eighteen years, yet here I am feeling guilty again. Only this time it's because everyone else is upset while I seem to be alone in thinking this is wonderful. If one more person says that it seems like only yesterday the girls were babies, I'll scream. Because, believe me, it isn't true.

I mean, people should be congratulating us *now*. Eighteen years ago, we didn't actually do anything special to get triplets. But now we've survived the sleepless nights, the never having enough arms and the sheer logistical nightmare of every trip out. And, despite all the problems, we've raised three gorgeous girls. So, you tell me why is everyone so miserable? Why are they afraid of letting go? The girls are ready to spread their wings and fly off to new adventures. This isn't the end of something, it's a bright new beginning.

And if this new beginning also means I get to watch what I want on TV, that any chocolate I buy will still be available for me to eat three hours later, and that I can stay in the bath for more than fifteen minutes without someone pounding on the door, so much the better. Just because I'm longing for some well-earned peace and quiet, it doesn't mean I don't love my daughters.

Lisa can't possibly understand what it's like to be a man in a house full of females. It wasn't so bad when the girls were small, but the older they got the more friends they accumulated. So instead of four females in the house, I suddenly had to contend with seven or eight. There were even twelve staying overnight on one occasion. Everywhere I looked there were giggling, sniggering groups of girls, and none of them appreciated having a man about the place. Do you know, I even had to get fully dressed to go to the bathroom.

'But daddy,' I was informed years ago, 'your dressing gown is *so embarrassing.*'

Ah, the thought of being able to wander freely through my own home, what bliss. I just wish Lisa could see it this way.

For her sake, it would be easier if the girls left separately. Then we could take Beth to Heathrow before her long flight to Perth, and we could take Natasha to University. But our girls aren't just sisters, they're triplets, and this is the way they want it to be. It's going to be hard watching them all drive away in Katie's car, but I'm guessing it's going to be just as hard, if not harder, for the girls to say goodbye to each other. They know their lives will never be the same again. None of our lives will ever be the same.

I glance around, the party's finally ending. I can tell this because now more than half the people are crying. Poor Lisa looks worse than ever. Heaven knows what she'll be like after the girls have gone tomorrow. I just hope I can show her how much I still love her and remind her of all the fun we used to have together before parenthood consumed all our energy. Personally, I can't wait.

Letting Go

Well, this is it, our last breakfast together. The girls are so excited they're all talking at once. For some reason I'm finding it hard to swallow my toast. They look so young. So vulnerable.

I look at Beth. She's off to a strange country. How can I protect her when she's so far away?

And what about Katie, alone in London. It's not that far from the Island, but that stretch of water means I can't just jump in the car and get to her quickly. And talking about cars, who's going to look after her car up there. I just know some garage will try and rip her off.

And didn't Natasha come running to me last year when that boy at school was pestering her. I'm not sure she's ready to handle a whole university of boys. Or worse… of men!

I watch as the last bags are forced into the boot. I put my arm around Lisa, I just know she's about to fall to pieces. Because the ferry is booked for eleven o'clock, we can't prolong our farewells, which is probably a good thing. Suddenly the moment has arrived.

'If you need anything at all, you know where we are. You only have to call,' I whisper to each of the girls as I give them one last hug. I wish I could hold them in my arms forever.

They tearfully promise to keep in touch as they climb in the car. Then, with waves and smiles, they're off.

Slowly we return to the kitchen. As usual, it looks like a hurricane has hit it. I slump in a chair while Lisa quickly clears the table.

'You know,' she says. 'For months I've been dreading this moment. But it's not so bad, is it? Of course I'll miss them, but do you realise how much less mess there's going to be? No more tidying up after them, much less shopping, cooking, and washing to do. Oh, Mike,' she laughs, as she dances round the kitchen. 'We're going to have so much free time. Isn't it wonderful?'

I look up at her.

'Oh, you big soppy thing,' she says, as she sits on my lap and gives me a cuddle. 'And I thought you couldn't wait for them to leave.'

'Me, want my babies to leave home,' I sob, as I grab a tissue and blow my nose. 'Whatever gave you that idea?'

The Holiday

I'd like to strangle the person who invented holidays. I bet it was a man. After all, they don't spend the preceding weeks washing clothes, sorting out suitcases, organising the pets, dealing with over-excited kids, all while working full time.

Take this morning, which everyone is laughingly referring to as the first day of *our* holiday. I was up at five-thirty. I've done the last bits of packing, made the sandwiches, cleaned the kitchen, lounge and bathroom. I've taken the key to our neighbour and the hamster to my mother's. I've piled the tents, sleeping bags, stove, suitcases and boxes of food by the front door.

What's my husband done? Simon sauntered out of bed around seven-thirty.

'Isn't it great not having to rush around,' he said.

The Holiday

I'm amazed he's still alive. And the boys aren't any better. Okay, Ryan's only seven and Jake's nine, but you'd think they could decide which games they're taking without quite so many arguments.

Finally, we're ready. As I climb in the car, the boys start squabbling over which film to watch on their tablet.

'Belt up!' I yell at them. They look shocked. I rephrase it slightly. 'Please put your seatbelts on,' I turn to Simon. 'Well, what are *you* waiting for?'

He opens his mouth to say something, then thinks better of it. He starts the car and we're off. Off to the sunny Isle of Wight. A place that has many hotels and guest houses. It also has caravans, which at a push would be acceptable. Unfortunately, it also has a lot of campsites. And that's where we're heading, to a campsite by the sea. No doubt camping is another male invention.

I know, I sound just like Ryan in one of his petulant moods. Oh god, do you think he's inherited it from me? Trouble was last year's holiday was a disaster. We went camping in Cornwall and it rained every day. I told Simon

The Holiday

this year I wanted to go to a hotel. I wanted to be pampered. Only we can't afford a hotel and, since Simon's firm lost their last contract, we're frightened to even spend the money on an Airbnb. So, to the delight of all the males in this family, it's a tent in a field... again. At least the weather forecast is looking good.

In fact, it's really hot and, as we hit the first traffic snarl-up, the heat in the car becomes almost unbearable. The air-con has packed up and Simon is too worried about spending the money to get it fixed. I try opening the windows, but the petrol fumes nearly choke us.

'Mum, I need the loo,' Jake says.

'We'll stop at the next service station,' I promise, and hope he doesn't realise it could take hours to get there.

'Mum, I feel sick,' adds Ryan.

I'm sick too – sick of the lot of them, but do I complain?

All the traffic delays mean we've missed our booked ferry, so we have a long wait until the next one. But once we are on, it's great standing on deck with the sun on my face and a nice sea breeze cooling me down. I try to forget the last five hours and the fifteen arguments it's taken to get us this far.

It's another two hours before we are finally at the campsite and in our allocated spot. I'm exhausted and as Simon starts to put up the tent, I decide the rest of us need to cool off.

'But we can go to a pool anytime,' whines Jake as we head towards the sports complex. 'I want to swim in the sea.'

I grit my teeth as we trek to the beach.

After our swim, we return to find Simon sitting back enjoying the sunshine. He points to the rest of the gear still in the car.

'Sorry, I didn't know where to stick it.'

I resist the temptation to tell him.

After I've sorted it all out, I flop in a chair.

'Mum, I'm hungry,' Jake complains.

'I'll cook,' Simon says.

What is it about men and cooking outdoors? He hardly ever helps in the kitchen. But far be it from me to discourage him, so I sit back while he massacres the meat.

The boys look suspiciously at the sausages on their plate. Black on the outside, raw on the inside. We decide to try the on-site cafeteria instead, where at least the food is edible.

The Holiday

'Mum, can we play in the amusement arcade?' Jake asks as he shovels down his last chip. Before I have a chance to reply, he's gone and Ryan follows. We sit and watch them in the next room arguing about which game to play.

'You don't look very happy,' Simon says, as he finishes off his burger.

'I'm just tired,' I say. Because that's what he wants to hear. He doesn't want to know that, given the choice, I'd rather be somewhere else. Even home would be preferable. At least I'd get to sleep in a bed.

Then I join the boys while Simon mysteriously goes to see someone. It's almost eight by the time we trudge back to the tents. Then they start fighting over the sleeping bags.

'Mine's the red one,' Ryan shouts.

'Yours is blue,' Jake argues.

I'm at screaming point when Simon reappears. He's happy and smelling of beer. I leave him with the boys and go outside.

'They want you to say goodnight,' he says two minutes later.

'I like this place,' Ryan mutters sleepily, as he puts his little arms around me. I kiss him. He's very sweet - shame I'm such a lousy mum.

The Holiday

And I have been horrible today. So I make up my mind that after what I hope will be a decent night's sleep, I'm going to wake up tomorrow and be cheerful. I'm going to enter into the spirit of this holiday, even if it kills me.

'We're going fishing, isn't that great?' Jake says, as I kiss him goodnight.

'Fishing!' I yell at my husband. 'You want me to spend my holiday fishing?'

'No, I'm taking the boys fishing, that's what I've been organising. We're going out for the next four mornings. I know it's not the same as being pampered, but you'll be able to lay on the beach without having to think about us. Because I do understand,' he adds, as he pulls me towards him, 'You need a break too.'

Then, as he tenderly runs his hands over my tired body, I begin to relax. As we lay on the sleeping bag, he starts to nibble my ear.

'I love you,' he whispers.

And I know, despite it all, I love him too. Maybe, just maybe, this holiday won't be so bad after all.

Touched By The Moon

I stood and watched as the demolition crew went about their work on the old seafront café. Along with the walls, I could see forty years of happy memories crumbling before my eyes. And it was all my fault, I should have tried harder to save the business.

'Amy, you're an accountant not a miracle worker,' Nick had said a year ago, when I'd finally finished my detailed analysis and told him the bad news. And of course he was right, but I still wished there could have been another way.

'I think your mum only kept the café going by ignoring the problems,' I'd explained back then. 'On the surface the café looks fine, but actually the building is in a terrible state. It needs a new roof, the windows are rotting, plus the extension is subsiding. It would cost a fortune, and since all the new parking restrictions have been put in place footfall in the café has dropped by nearly 75%. There's no way we can afford to keep it going.'

If Nick was upset, he didn't show it. Even today he was laughing and joking with the contractors as a big piece of our history was wiped from existence. I couldn't watch anymore. With tears in my eyes, I turned and walked away.

I'd been seven years old the first time my grandmother had taken me to the café. It was before the extension had been added, so was a lot smaller and the menu had been very basic, but I loved the place. Gran would either buy me an ice lolly or an orange squash, except on a Fridays if Gramps had worked overtime the week before. Then I'd be treated to a knickerbocker glory with extra cream. It was my idea of heaven.

I'm not really sure why my grandparents moved to the Isle of Wight, I just knew that the first summer holidays they lived there, I was packed off to stay with them the whole six weeks. My dad hadn't been well, and Mum had to work full time. I'd been so excited to visit as I'd been told that they'd moved close to the sea, which I'd assumed meant I'd get to spend the whole time on the beach.

Only when I arrived, I discovered that it was only in my imagination that every bit of the sea had gentle waves which washed onto glorious sandy beaches. It did do that in some parts of the Island, but not near my grandparent's house. The sea near them simply pounded against a dirty grey stonewall. Occasionally the tide would go out far enough to reveal a narrow strip of rocks. I didn't understand why there wasn't sand, or why the rocks always showed up at different times of the day.

Gramps tried to explain it to me. I wasn't impressed, at least not until he told me about the moon and how it affected the sea. How its powerful forces touched each and every one of us. I was fascinated. In the evenings, I would drag Gran and Gramps down to the seafront to watch the moon cast its shadow across the water.

During the day, Gran and I would walk all the way to the café, where Gran would buy us drinks and I'd sit studying the sea as it moved in and out. Mostly our walks were confined to the pavement but, when the tide was low, Gran allowed me to go down on the so-called beach.

In the watery rock pools, she'd point out all the tiny life that also depended on the moon and the tides.

The following year my mother was still working, although Dad was getting stronger. I was sent to the Island, both at Easter and for the summer holidays and I couldn't have been happier.

Even after Dad was much better, I would beg my parents to let me spend my holidays on the Island, especially after I'd met Nick. His parents owned the small café and about three years after I'd first visited, they'd added the extension and turned it into a proper café. Then it sold lots of fizzy drinks, six flavours of ice cream, four flavours of milkshakes, and such a large selection of cakes that poor Gran would have to go and sit down while I spent ten minutes deciding which one to have.

Nick was twelve. Tall for his age with light brown wavy hair and a smile that lit up my ten-year-old world. He'd help his mum clear the dirty tables and do some of the washing up. He always chatted to Gran and me.

Every day that summer I asked to walk along the seafront as far as the café. I said it was to feed the seagulls, and darling Gran never complained. But she did always insist that I count and identify the birds that came flocking for our bread. I regularly counted over fifty, and I'm sure it was during those hot hazy days that I fell in love with numbers – not to mention my crush on Nick.

The next few years followed a similar pattern. I'd arrive at the start of my holidays and the first thing I'd want to do was go for a walk to the seafront café. Nick and the café seemed to grow up together. By the time I was thirteen it sold frothy coffee and did proper meals, and Nick had gone from a fun-loving friend to a sullen, spotty teenager who ignored girls. Suddenly the days weren't quite so sunny, but it never stopped me staying with Gran.

When I was sixteen, I got a summer job at the café. I enjoyed waitressing and chatting to the locals, plus the money was useful. Nick's spots had disappeared along with his shyness, and that summer we spent our evenings watching the moon as it hung magically over the sea.

I understood how our silvery satellite affected the planet, but I didn't understand why its soft white light affected me so much. I was just relieved that Nick felt it too. When we finally kissed, it was standing in the moonlight on that rocky shoreline with the waves lapping close to our feet.

That was a glorious six weeks, but it ended all too soon. I went back home to learn accountancy and Nick started working for an engineering company far away up north. It was ten years before I saw him again.

During that time life was busy. Gramps died, and Gran moved up closer to my parents before deciding she didn't like being away from the Island. So she returned and moved into a newly built retirement complex just around the corner from where she used to live.

I was only able to visit for the odd weekend, and I so missed those long, lazy summers of my childhood, but whenever I stayed, the first thing we did was take a walk along the seafront to the café. I still loved sitting there, staring out at the water.

Sometimes the calm sea would glisten in the bright sunlight. At other times, the wind would make a hundred white horses dance across its surface. When it rained, I'd drive us to the café where we'd sit inside, drink hot chocolate and chat with Nick's mum.

I was twenty-six when Gran died. The night before her funeral, I walked to the café alone. It was late and the place was closed, but I stood against the wall remembering all the wonderful times Gran had given me. I was surprised when Nick suddenly appeared.

'I'm so sorry, Amy,' he said.

'She enjoyed her life,' I replied tearfully. Then he opened up the café, led me inside and made me a coffee. It's hard to believe that was twenty-five years ago.

'You ran off before the demolition had finished,' Nick said, puffing slightly as he caught me up.

'You're covered in brick-dust,' I replied, as I brushed bits of café off his jacket.

He smiled and pulled me into his arms.

'I know it's going to seem strange without the old place, but Mum would be pleased with what we're doing,' he tried to reassure me.

'Would she? That café was her life, and I've just turned it into a pile of rubble.'

'You did what you've always done and made a sensible business decision. She'd understand that. Besides, we're not destroying anything; we're about to build our beautiful new home on the café's land.'

Deep down I knew he was right, the happy times at the café will always be with me, locked securely in my memory. Now it was time we moved on to the next phase.

We've been given permission to build us a home on the site. Somewhere for our own grandchildren to come and stay. Somewhere safe and warm for another generation to watch as the tides continue to ebb and flow. For them to explore the creatures in the rock pools, and for us to teach them about the magic of the moon as it controls the sea and gently lights up all our lives.

Tinsel and Turkey

I looked at my grandmother to see if she was joking. Unfortunately, she looked very serious and very pleased with herself. Surely she knew how much I hated turkey, and I'd never been big on tinsel either.

'So,' I said slowly, wanting to get the facts absolutely correct. 'You've already booked for me to come with you?'

She proudly waved the ticket at me.

'Melanie love, a breakaway is just what you need to cheer you up after all the upset. You've always been enthusiastic about my Tinsel and Turkey weeks on the Isle of Wight, so this is my early Christmas present to you.'

'I don't know what to say,' I muttered truthfully. I suppose I could have told her that encouraging her to go off on coach trips was a whole lot different from wanting to go on one myself, but I didn't.

'And you've often said you fancied visiting the Island,' she reminded me.

Hmm, so I had. But I'd pictured lazing on the beaches in July, not pulling crackers in some freezing hotel at the end of November. I'd never been a particularly Christmassy sort of person and, after all that had happened recently, I was dreading this one. So, a week-long dress rehearsal a month before the event was the last thing I needed.

It used to be that these festive breaks were confined to the month of December, but it seemed hotels were following the shops and starting earlier and earlier. I really didn't want this, but I knew Nan was only trying to help. If there was an easy or tactful way to get out of this trip without hurting her feelings, then I wasn't quick enough to think it up in the space of a few minutes.

'Thank you,' I said, giving her a big hug.

I left her looking extremely happy, so at least my selfless act wasn't in vain. Maybe going away with a group of pensioners for a week was better than staying at home moping, and you could get some sunshine in November, if you were lucky.

Tinsel and Turkey

We weren't. Ten days later, I was sitting on the ferry watching the rain pounding against the windows. The sea was rough, but that didn't stop everyone tucking into tea and sticky buns. I was by far the youngest person in our group, and from the way most of the folks were fussing over me you'd have thought I was nine, not twenty-nine. Nan was even reading me the itinerary for the next few days. A trip to Cowes, a tour of Carisbrooke Castle, a day at Osborne House to see where Queen Victoria had lived, and several Christmas shopping expeditions.

'Isn't that exciting dear,' she said, patting my hand.

'I'm sure it'll be great,' I agreed, forcing a smile.

I knew my family didn't really understand why I was so upset at losing my job. In their eyes I had good qualifications and could easily get another position. They were probably right, but I'd worked for the same firm since university, and to find it was suddenly merging with a rival company and that several of us were now surplus to requirements was a terrible shock.

It was also a shock to discover that, since I'd dedicated so much time to my career, I didn't have a life outside of work. All my friends were married with children which, according to my mother, was what I should be.

Of course I'd been out on plenty of dates over the years, but there had only been one proper relationship, and that had broken up when he'd been promoted and needed to move four hundred miles away to Scotland. I'd refused to give up my job and go with him. As neither of us was prepared to compromise, we'd gone our separate ways.

Not that I regretted it, but I did now find myself floating loose in a strange world without a sense of identity. I was no longer someone with a challenging career and excellent prospects. I'd already started applying for other positions, but for the moment it felt as if I didn't belong anywhere. Especially not on this ferry with a load of chatty women who thought a week of tinsel and turkey was a great idea.

The rain had eased by the time we docked, which meant I could see a little of the scenery as we drove across the Island. It did look pretty. The hotel was the same one Nan always stayed in, and she'd told me it was directly opposite the beach – not that I'd bothered packing my bikini.

The light was already fading when we stepped off the coach, and I was expecting the place to look bleak and barren. Instead, the rugged beauty took my breath away. I stared at the wild, powerful waves as they crashed onto the beach. The air was fresh and clean, and I could taste the salt in the breeze as it whipped past me. I had this sudden urge to drop everything and run along the sand, unfortunately Nan chose that moment to grab my arm and pull me inside.

The hotel foyer had an oversized, gaudy Christmas tree in the corner. Everywhere else seemed covered with balloons, banners and baubles, not to mention masses of the dreaded tinsel. For a moment, I had visions of the turkey I'd be forced to eat at every mealtime, and I desperately wanted to go home.

The next hour passed in a haze of luggage sorting and key allocating, but eventually we found ourselves in a comfortably sized room. I walked across to the window and, as I looked out at the magnificent view of the darkening sea, I felt an unfamiliar sense of peace sweep over me. Perhaps this wasn't such a terrible idea after all.

We freshened up before joining the rest of the party for afternoon tea. They were mainly women from one of Nan's clubs, and everyone knew each other. They did try to include me in their conversations, but when Brenda started giving a detailed account of her recent operation, I slipped outside.

It was now dark, but the streetlights made the beach look even more inviting. I stuck my hands in my pockets to stop them freezing and went for a walk. I'd hoped the biting wind would blow away all the unwanted thoughts in my head, but it didn't. I was still asking myself the same questions. Why hadn't I seen the merger coming? Why hadn't my boss, who I'd always admired and trusted, warned me? I thought I was good at judging people and situations. How could I have been so wrong?

Before I sank too far into the depths of self-pity, I went back to the hotel. Despite the overabundance of decorations, the place was warm with a homely feel, and I was even happier to be there when I discovered turkey wasn't on tonight's menu.

There was music playing in the main lounge that evening, and while Nan played

Scrabble with her friends, I spent most of my time staring out at the sea and the stars. It was very relaxing.

The next morning, we all traipsed onto the coach for a trip to Carisbrooke Castle. It was a brighter day and the views as I walked around the top walls of the castle were amazing. I could see why my grandmother loved the place, although why she didn't come in the warmer weather I had no idea.

Everyone on the trip was friendly and over lunch I got chatting to a nice couple who'd known my grandmother a long time. They also knew all about me losing my job.

'I was made redundant three times before I retired,' the chap told me. 'It just seems to be part and parcel of working life these days.'

I wasn't sure that made me feel any better.

We arrived back at the hotel just after four, and I left them all chatting happily in the lounge, while I went for another wander along the beach. I sat in the dark for a while and listened to the waves. For a moment all my problems seemed to disappear. Then I checked my phone and found I had two job application rejections in my inbox. My redundancy package had been generous, so it wasn't as if I needed to find another position immediately, but the fact that no one even wanted to interview me felt like another kick in the teeth. The dark sea suddenly didn't look so appealing.

When I got back to the hotel, I saw Pete Anderson standing in reception looking harassed. He was about five years older than me and had recently taken over the running of the hotel from his mother. I knew this because Nan had given me his full family history the night before, proving that she'd been visiting this place for far too many years.

'But there must be someone on your books you can send. I have a hotel full of guests and no one to serve them dinner.'

He wasn't exactly shouting down the phone, but he did sound desperate. I watched as he ran a hand through his curly brown hair, he looked ready to pull it out poor man.

'Yes, I understand, but if you can find me some people in the morning, I'd be very grateful. Even if it's just one person it'll help.'

I wasn't quite sure what to do. Lurking by the Christmas tree listening to his conversation seemed rude, but he obviously had a problem and walking away seemed equally inappropriate.

He only noticed me as he put down the phone and he instantly pasted on a smile.

'Can I help you?' he asked.

'No, but I might be able to help you,' I replied.

At first he was reluctant to admit anything, but one thing I was good at was getting the truth out of people.

'Finding reliable staff is the biggest problem in this business,' he admitted. 'I was already down to the minimum because a girl quit last week without notice. Now poor Sheila's fractured her arm this afternoon and her daughter, who always helps me in emergencies, is at the hospital with her. Also, my mother and aunt are normally around, only they're currently sunning themselves in Australia for a month.'

I felt so sorry for him. Seems he could manage the cooking but couldn't see how to get the food to the tables without it going cold.

'I'm not an expert,' I said. 'But I did work in a cafe part time when I was at university.'

Bless him, he was still protesting that it wasn't the done thing to have guests waiting tables as I began carrying out the starters. But he wasn't stupid either, he knew he didn't have any other options. As for me, I found waiting on tables in the dining room much more fun than sitting at them. Plus, Pete was serving turkey tonight, so I figured being in the kitchen might mean I could find something different to eat.

I was surprised Nan didn't protest more about me offering to help, but strangely enough she was all for it and didn't moan once about me being a workaholic. Which was a first. Anyway, it didn't feel like work. It was great chatting to the folk as I served them and, after the last few weeks, it felt even better being useful and needed again.

Pete said I wasn't to help clear up after dinner, but I ignored him.

'You'll be up half the night otherwise,' I pointed out as I loaded the big commercial dishwasher for the second time.

It was almost ten before we finished laying up the dining room for breakfast.

'Thank you so much, Melanie,' he said, as he picked up a bottle of brandy. 'I think we deserve a nightcap.'

Which was how come I spent the next two hours with him. He was good company, and so easy to talk to. I even found myself telling him all my problems, as if the poor guy didn't have enough of his own.

Nan was still awake when I crept into our room just after midnight.

'Sorry, I didn't mean to disturb you,' I whispered.

'You aren't disturbing me sweetie,' she replied cheerfully. 'Pete is a dear, isn't he? Did I tell you he gave up his career at sea when his dad became ill? He's been such a support to Rosemary, his mother. But she worries that he works too hard and has no time to find himself a girlfriend.'

'How do you know all this if you only visit here once a year?' I asked, as I slipped on my nightdress.

'Oh, Rosemary and I have become good friends over the years. We email each other regularly. You and Pete have a lot in common,' she added before saying goodnight.

If I hadn't been so tired, I might have spent more time wondering if I'd been brought on this trip for reasons other than the fresh salty air. As it was, I fell asleep almost instantly. Something I'd not been able to do for years.

The agency did find someone the next morning, but not before I'd helped Pete with the breakfasts. Lucy was just eighteen and hadn't a clue what to do. She was willing but needed supervising. So there I was, faced with a dilemma - did I stay at the hotel and help with the cleaning, or did I get on the coach and attempt to enjoy being dragged around shops who thought customers enjoyed listening to 'Jingles Bells' in November?

Vacuuming can be so relaxing on occasions, don't you think?

When it was all finished, Pete made me some lunch and we sat by a window looking out over the sea.

'You're so lucky being able to have this view every day,' I said. 'When I was working, I used to grab a sandwich at my desk. It had a wonderful view of a blank wall. My flat has a view of a Chinese takeaway and charity shop. I envy you this fresh air too.'

'I guess sometimes I take all this for granted,' he said. 'It's nice when someone reminds me what a privilege it is to live in such a beautiful place.'

Then he started to tell me about the changes he wanted to make to the hotel now he was in control.

'I'm putting in for permission to extend the place. I want to enclose the outdoor swimming pool and make it into a small leisure complex. I'm hoping it will encourage the locals to use the hotel out of season.'

He had some great ideas, and he even showed me the sketches he'd done. He was full of enthusiasm, and it did all sound exciting.

Later, as I helped Lucy serve up the tea and biscuits to the happy trippers on their return, I realised how much I was enjoying myself. I'd worked for so many years in a stress-filled environment where everything had to be done yesterday, that I'd forgotten people could take the time to sit and talk to each other.

Two days later Sheila's daughter came in to work, but even with Lucy that still left Pete short-staffed. So, I cleverly offered to carry on serving dinner in the evenings, which meant I could still avoid the turkey.

Unfortunately, that left me free to resume the coach tours. We spent a few hours being drizzled on while wandering around some villages, before being taken to a garden centre. It had a lot of singing Santas, a mass of flashing plastic trees and what looked like enough coloured lights to decorate every house on the Island.

'It's a garden centre for heaven's sake! Why can't I find any plants?' I moaned.

'I reckon you would have been happier staying behind and helping Pete,' Nan said. 'And you should have done, I wouldn't have minded, you know.'

'He didn't need my help,' I replied. Just why was I here on this holiday? My family never normally interfered in my life, and I suppose Nan wasn't exactly interfering now, but I did feel I was being nudged in a certain direction. Not that I needed her encouragement. The more time I spent with Pete, the more I liked him.

Later that evening, as I was helping him lay up for breakfast, he asked me if I'd like to see the architects with him the following day.

'He's coming here about eleven and you made a couple of great suggestions regarding the layout of the changing rooms. Plus, it would be nice to have someone else's input.' Then he added, 'You do seem to be very good at problem solving, Mel.'

Well, it was easy solving other people's problems. It was just my own that I had trouble with.

'I'd love to see the architect with you,' I replied. Being wanted was such a boost for my battered ego. Being wanted by Pete somehow boosted it even further. I couldn't help noticing he looked very happy with my answer, I also noticed how happy I felt. Funny, but this trip wasn't turning out at all as I'd expected.

The next morning, everyone happily climbed aboard the coach leaving me and Pete to our meeting. We both came away from it full of ideas, and then spent most of the afternoon discussing all the possibilities.

However, it wasn't until after dinner the following evening, that we found the time to sit and discuss the expansion in more detail. We'd been doing this for a couple of hours when Pete suddenly popped the question.

I just stared at him for a moment.

'Are you offering me a job?'

He looked hopeful, yet very uncertain at the same time.

'Sort of,' he replied. 'But it's more that I'd like you to work with me, rather than work for me. I can only imagine the sort of salary you've been earning in the city, so you'll probably see this as an insult. But even though we've only known each other a week, I have this feeling we'd make a great team.' Then he added, 'And there are worse places to live than on the Isle of Wight.'

Had I only known this lovely man for such short a time? It seemed way longer. But this was such a drastic change of career, and he was right, I had been earning very good money. Of course, I'd also been paying an extortionate rent and the fares for my commute had been eye-watering. I still wasn't sure if it was a good or a bad thing that what money I had left over was mainly still in the bank, because who had time to go and spend it – certainly I hadn't.

Moving to the Island to help run a hotel would be a massive change, but there wasn't anyone waiting for me back home. Certainly nobody who would look at me with… what was that I could see in his eyes? Whatever it was, it made my heart beat faster.

I couldn't answer Pete immediately, so I got up and walked over to the window. The moon was bright in the sky, and I could see its reflection in the water. Even with his offer overwhelming me, the sight of the sea calmed me. After a while I turned and looked at him.

'So, Pete, knowing how I feel about tinsel, you really want me to stay here surrounded by the stuff?'

'Hey, it's only up for a few weeks each year, I promise I pack it away in January,' he laughed. Then he added, 'Plus if you stay, I can assure you Mel, I'll never make you eat turkey whatever time of the year it is.'

And if that wasn't enough to persuade me to stay, then the way he came over, took me in his arms and kissed me certainly was.

Nan was delighted when I told her.

'But the hotel is closing for the whole of January, so I haven't committed myself past December,' I explained. 'Both Pete and I think it's a good idea to see how things go over the next few weeks before making any final decisions.'

'Very sensible,' she agreed.

However, later on I overheard her telling one of her friends that Pete and I were probably going to be getting married. So not sure what part of taking things slowly she didn't understand. And, judging by a text Pete got from his mother, it sounded like Nan was telling her the same thing.

Just before Nan left the following day, I gave her a list of things I wanted sent from home. Did she look upset to leave her favourite granddaughter behind? No, she just looked smug at what I assumed she felt was her excellent matchmaking skills.

Pete and I stood side by side as we waved and watched the coach disappear.

'Not having any regrets,' he asked.

'None so far.' I replied as I looked at this rather lovely man and his rather lovely beach.

Then we had to jump to it, because the next coach party was due in a few hours and there was a lot to do. Although we did find time for one more rather lovely kiss.

The Perfect Place

I was twenty, the war was just over, and I was living with my parents and two sisters in a tiny two up two down in the centre of the Isle of Wight. I was happy in my job, and I was in love. Harry was twenty-five and the man of my dreams. Even though he was just average height with mousy hair and hard to describe eyes, I loved his smile, his sense of humour and the fact he had plans.

'Emma, I want us to be together and live in the perfect place.'

I'd laugh at that because I felt perfection was a tall order. Besides I was young, and I didn't care where I lived, as long as it with was with my Harry. Or I didn't think I cared.

Six months before our wedding, Harry came rushing to meet me from work.

'I've found it. I've found us the perfect place,' he shouted excitedly.

The Perfect Place

I was more relieved than anything, especially as I didn't fancy starting married life at his mother's. She was nice enough, but she lacked anything resembling a sense of humour. I had no idea what to expect from Harry's perfect place, but in my head anything had to be better than sharing a bedroom with my two younger sisters.

I went along to see it with him feeling so happy. That feeling didn't last long. Surely a "Perfect Place" was supposed to be well... perfect? Surely it wasn't supposed to be a complete wreck.

'It's just a little bomb damaged,' Harry assured me, as I stood looking at a little cottage that was as far from perfect as I reckoned you could get without it falling down.

'Remember, both Dad and I are structural engineers, it won't take long to repair these cracked walls. And replacing the roof and broken windows will be easy.'

'There isn't any electricity,' I pointed out, as I picked my way through the rubble.

'That's no problem to fix,' he said confidently. 'And Uncle Bill can install running water and a toilet.'

The Perfect Place

I did try to match his enthusiasm, but it wasn't easy.

'How long will it take to do it up?' I asked.

'It'll be liveable by the wedding,' he promised. 'Don't you worry Emma, it'll be perfect when it's finished.'

Well, one room was liveable by the wedding, and the outside toilet had been repaired enough to be working – most of the time. Good job I was too much in love to object to the brick dust or the buckets needed every time it rained. But Harry was right, the little cottage was great when he'd finished. It did take him two years, and our baby was six months by then, but I was very happy.

I was also proud of the fact that I'd done a lot of the decorating, and I'd completely transformed the back garden. In fact, I was sitting out there reading to little Alice, when Harry came rushing in one day.

'Emma, you've got to see this. I've found us the perfect place,' he shouted.

Being pregnant again, I was excited at the idea of having a bigger home, especially a perfect one. Which, with hindsight, was probably a bit optimistic of me.

The Perfect Place

Harry took me to a house opposite the park.

'It's a lovely location,' I agreed. 'But it's only got two bedrooms the same as we have now.'

Which is when he told me how easy it would be to remove the roof and add another floor.

'See, the house down the road has done the same.' He was so excited, and he did make it sound simple.

I suppose, compared to the first house, it wasn't too bad. After all, we did have electricity and running water. Harry didn't start working on it until a month after the baby was born, and I was amazed how long you could live in a house without a roof. I even got used to brick dust infiltrating every nook and cranny, although I never grew to like it.

Harry and his dad were busy at proper paid work, which was why progress on our house was so slow. By the time it was finished, Alice was at school, and baby number three had arrived. I was so relieved when finally we had a house that didn't need cleaning every single day. I told Harry my idea of perfection was to stay in that house for the rest of my life.

The Perfect Place

Some hopes! Four years of blissful cleanliness was all I had.

'Oh, Emma, you are going to love this, I've found us the perfect place,' he said one bright summer's day. My heart plummeted, but the more he described the place, the more enthusiastic I became.

'The garden is huge, and it backs onto a small copse. The beach is just a short walk away. It'll be the perfect place for our kids to play.'

It did sound idyllic, but I knew Harry rather well by now.

'What's the catch?' I asked.

He grinned as he pulled me closer and gave me a long, lingering kiss. Which I guessed meant the place would only be perfect after a *lot* of work.

'You've got to be joking,' I cried, the moment we arrived. 'Harry, it's just a shack. There's no way I'm moving into this.'

'It's a very large shack,' he pointed out. 'And we'll only need to live in it until we build the house.'

Harry had always longed to design and build his own home, but decent plots were expensive. However, this wasn't a plot as such, just a tatty old shack in a large garden. The current owner had lived there for years. It looked like he'd started with a small shed and, over time, had added further shed-like rooms. It was now like a mini maze with doors, windows and makeshift corridors in the oddest of places. The kitchen, with its cast iron sink and uneven flagstone flooring, looked like it belonged in a Charles Dickens' novel. But it did have a working bathroom, which Harry seemed to think would make up for everything else.

I did love him, but even I had to admit he had some very strange ideas.

'The shack just needs a few repairs, a coat of paint and some floor covering, and it'll be fine for the short time it takes to build the house,' Harry assured me, proving he'd given this a lot of thought

'Just how "short" a time are we talking?' I asked. 'And be realistic, Harry.'

He looked a bit sheepish as he muttered two years.

'It took longer than that to put the extra floor on our current house,' I reminded him.

'But there will be more people working on this,' he said. 'Honestly Em, even with getting the planning permission, it shouldn't take more than three.'

Three years living in a shack, in the middle of a building plot. Who wouldn't want to give up a nice comfortable home for that?

'Let's go explore the gardens before you make up your mind,' he said, as he took my hand.

I was about to tell him my mind was already made up, when he took me past the smelly chicken enclosure and I saw it. It was a gardener's dream. Apart from the amazing amount of space, there was also a little stream running through a bluebell carpeted wooded area at the bottom of the garden. There was a tiny orchard with half a dozen apple trees, three plum trees and a pear tree. The centrepiece of the garden itself was a wonderful old copper beech tree.

'Oh Harry, it's beautiful,' I gasped.

'I know,' he said proudly, as if he'd conjured it up all by himself. 'The kids will love it.'

He helped me climb over a decaying wooden gate, and into the wooded area beyond. Then we had about a five-minute walk to the beach. It wasn't the sandiest of beaches on the

Isle of Wight but then it didn't get a lot of visitors, so that was a plus. Harry was right; this was a perfect spot for children.

'But they aren't going to like living in a shack any more than I am,' I pointed out.

He just grinned and said, 'Why don't we ask them?'

I'd forgotten my children had their father's genes. The boys thought living there was a fantastic idea. Alice loved that her bedroom had its own door to the garden. Even the dog made it plain he wanted to stay.

I was well and truly outvoted, and four months later there I was packing everything up and we were on the move again.

The shack was all I'd expected it to be. Freezing cold in the winter, a nightmare to cook in and impossible to keep clean the rest of the time.

'It'll all be worth it,' Harry would promise, as I was washing yet another load of mud-covered clothes or making yet more mugs of tea for the workmen.

And it was. We took up residence two days before Alice's twelfth birthday. Harry had done us proud. My kitchen was gorgeous, the children had a bedroom each, and the lounge had large patio doors that opened onto the garden. I'd been working hard on that for a while, and it was now a mixture of lawn, flowerbeds and wild play areas. Even I had to admit it was the perfect place to live.

We organised a big barbeque on the day the old shack was demolished. I thought I'd be pleased to see the hideous place smashed to pieces, but actually it was rather sad. It had been our home for over four years, and we'd had a lot of laughs in it.

Harry replaced it with a double garage which, for another year or so, created more brick dust for me to clear up, but he did promise that was the end of the work.

Thirty years later, and the grandchildren all look horrified when I show them photos of the old shack.

'You really lived in that?'

Even I had problems believing it now.

'Well, you know your Granddad,' I laughed. 'Never happy unless he's knocking down a wall or putting up an extension.'

The Perfect Place

They did know. Harry might have left our place alone, but he never stopped tinkering with the homes of our children. And, for some reason, I always seemed to be the one helping clear up his mess afterwards. Perhaps because I'd had so much practice.

We'd just celebrated our fiftieth wedding anniversary when Harry hurried into the house and shouted, 'Emma, I've found us the perfect place.' Well, when I say hurried, he went as fast as he could with his dodgy hip.

The grandchildren were off to university, and the days of little ones playing in our wonderland garden were long gone, as was my energy for keeping it up together.

I happily went with Harry to look at the retirement complex they'd just finished building in the centre of town. The flats were compact, but there was a large communal room, and a restaurant attached.

'Imagine moving into a place where we don't have to do anything,' I said excitedly.

'I was thinking, if I knocked down the wall between the second bedroom and the lounge we'd have a much bigger room,' Harry replied.

'Oh, Em, you should see your face, I was only joking,' he laughed.

I have no idea whether he was or not at the time but, two years later, he did just that. I moaned a lot, especially as I was clearing up the mess. But he was right, it was now a much better size for our first great-granddaughter to run around in.

The family threw a party for Harry's eighty-fifth birthday. He'd been in hospital earlier that year, and we were all pleased to see him back to his old self again.

A couple of weeks later he went out on his own and came back with a grin on his face. He had more wrinkles and less hair, but he was still the best-looking chap I knew.

'What have you been up to?' I asked.

'I've only found us the perfect place,' he declared.

'But we're happy here,' I cried.

'Of course we are. I don't mean for now.'

With all his old enthusiasm, he led me to the car and drove for fifteen minutes, still refusing to tell me where we were going. Then he turned down a lane and into a small car park.

The Perfect Place

Hand in hand, we walked through an archway and into the woodland cemetery.

There were chaffinches and blackbirds singing as we walked along the path. Then we saw three beautiful red squirrels playing between the trees as Harry stopped by a plot.

'It's so pretty and peaceful here. I thought that one day this would make a lovely last home for us, a place we can be together forever,' he said. 'What do you think?'

I think my husband can never stop planning. But as I looked around at the breathtaking views, I had to agree. However, there was something missing.

'Harry, you realise there are no walls here for you to knock down.'

'I think I can cope with that,' he laughed, as he slipped his arm around me.

Oh yes, eternity with Harry and no brick dust, now that was my idea of perfection. As I cuddled up to the man I'd loved for so long, I said, 'You're right Harry, one day this will be the perfect place for us, but hopefully not for a few years yet.'

Mayday, Mayday, Mayday!

Teresa's hands were trembling as she started pressing the buttons on the radio.

'Mayday, Mayday, Mayday,' she shouted far too loudly into the hand mike. She took a deep breath and tried to calm herself down a little before continuing. 'This is yacht Silver Lining, Silver Lining, Silver Lining. Mayday, this is yacht Silver Lining. We have struck rocks and are starting to sink…'

Teresa knew she was supposed to give more information, but what? Her mind had gone completely blank. Oh, why had she ever thought she could do this? Why had she ever thought this was a good idea? She'd never been good in stressful situations, it was one of the reasons she'd never wanted to learn to sail. Her husband loved the sea, but Teresa knew it was a dangerous place. Deep dark waters and damned great booms hurtling from side to side just waiting to hit you around the head. Whoever thought that made a good combination?

Land was where she felt safest, so why had she let her husband talk her into this? Teresa stared at the radio. Her mouth was dry, and her hands were horribly sweaty. Her position. She had to tell them her position.

'We are fifty degrees forty-six minutes north, one degree seventeen minutes west. We require immediate assistance. There are two people on board, one injured. Over.'

As Teresa released the speak button, she tried to go over what she'd just said. Had she given all the information they needed? It was one thing reading how to deal with emergencies while sitting on her comfy sofa at home, but this was very different.

As she sat on the wooden seat waiting for a reply, she couldn't help wishing she was at home right now. Why wasn't she tucked up in her nice warm kitchen with a pot of tea and some chocolate hobnobs?

Teresa had been married to Dave for almost thirty years, and he'd always been a keen dinghy sailor but, until recently, he'd never tried to persuade her to join him in his hobby.

Mayday, Mayday, Mayday

Over the years, she'd actively encouraged him to teach their two boys to sail. She'd happily spent many hot summer Sundays lazing on shore watching as the males in her life pitted their wits against sea, wind and the other crazy sailors. On their return, she'd had no problems listening as they'd explained in great detail how they'd cleverly won the race, or how it wasn't their fault they'd lost it.

It was an arrangement that had served her well, except now the boys were living at the other end of the country and poor old Dave was complaining he could no longer race competitively against a bunch of twenty-year-olds. Which was when he'd come up with the idea of buying a nice little thirty-two-foot cruising yacht to sail in his old age. Teresa had been delighted and had backed him all the way, right up until the point he'd asked her to sail it with him.

She jumped as the radio crackled and her Mayday call was acknowledged. She pressed her speak button again and gave a mumbled thanks. All she could do now was wait.

Teresa remembered the day Dave had first shown her around the boat.

'Believe me, we'll have fun together,' Dave had insisted, as he'd tried to convince her that anyone could sail this boat. Even her.

'And if you get used to it now, when we've retired in a few years, we can take six months out to sail around the British coastline. Can you imagine it?' he'd asked.

As she'd looked around the boat, she could imagine it all too well. The main bedroom was miniscule and mainly consisted of an odd-shaped bed. Whoever slept next to the wall would have to scramble over the top of the other person to get out in the middle of the night. Very friendly! The shower was the size of her airing cupboard at home, and as for trying to cook on that tiny stove, well he could forget that.

And if it felt claustrophobic down below, it was nothing to the nightmare of being on deck. The sails whipped about viciously in the wind, the boat creaked constantly and the sound of the rigging slapping against the mast gave her a headache. Even moored in the marina the water tossed the boat around like it was an insignificant leaf. The only water Teresa was comfortable in was hot, bubbly and in a bath.

Ignoring her reluctance, Dave didn't give up. 'Teresa, this boat isn't like my old dinghy, it wouldn't throw you in the water if you do something wrong. All you'll have to do on board is sit in the sun and pretend it's a luxury liner.'

Despite telling him she didn't have that good an imagination, she finally gave in. It was plain this meant a great deal to her husband, so she agreed on one condition.

'If we're going out on this boat together, then I need to know what I'm doing,' she told him. 'Just in case you have an accident.'

Dave had snorted at the idea of him being incapable of bringing them home safely.

'You worry too much,' he said, but she noticed he didn't stop her enrolling on a few courses.

Teresa glanced at her watch; five minutes since the acknowledgment of her Mayday message. What on earth was taking so long?

It was another three minutes before she saw the guy heading towards her.

'Congratulations Teresa,' he said with a smile. 'You had full marks for your written paper, and although you didn't get the Mayday message in quite the right order, it's good enough for a pass.'

It was! Thank heavens for that. With a massive sigh of relief, Teresa thanked her examiner and gratefully accepted her certificate. Somehow, she felt that sailing with Dave couldn't be anywhere near as stressful as having to pass this radio exam.

As she walked back to her car, Teresa started to smile. She'd now completed several courses and felt far more confident on the water. Even the yacht was more comfortable since she'd rearranged a few things.

She was still rather iffy about sailing around Britain when they retired, but she had agreed to starting on something smaller. In June they were going to join loads of other boats and sail around the Isle of Wight. And suddenly she didn't feel quite so worried about it all. Not now that she was fully qualified to call for help should they ever need it.

Golden Opportunity

'This is a complete disaster,' I sighed as I waded through the murky, foul-smelling water that was slopping around my shop.

'Try looking at it as more of an inconvenience than a disaster,' the fireman said with an encouraging smile. 'Remember what they say, problems are simply opportunities waiting to be taken.'

'Very philosophical,' I snapped. 'Perhaps you'll try telling that to my bank when it demands to know why I'm not paying off my overdraft.'

'I know this flood is lousy timing for you,' he agreed. 'But you'll soon get it sorted. It's not as bad as it looks, honest.'

If that was supposed to reassure me, it didn't. I'd been due to open the door of this scary new venture in twenty minutes, instead I was standing ankle-deep in dirty water. Exactly where was the opportunity in that?

'Come on, Fran. There's nothing more you can do in here. The pumps are working, so the water level will soon start to go down.' The fireman put a gentle but firm arm around me and guided me out of the shop.

Despite his dumb platitudes, he was just the sort of guy to have around in an emergency. He was so cool and calm, and he had stopped me going to pieces and making things worse. Although, I wasn't exactly sure how my situation could be any worse.

Outside it was still chucking it down with rain, but as I was already soaked it hardly mattered. As I stepped onto the pavement, I could see lights in all the nearby premises.

'Is mine the only shop to be flooded?' I asked.

'Yours is the closest to the blocked drain, and the only one slightly below ground level,' he explained. I took that to mean yes.

I wanted to scream about how unfair life was, but that hardly went with the image of a young, sophisticated businesswoman, which was what I was trying to fool people into thinking I was.

A Golden Opportunity

Despite the rain, there were still a crowd of on-lookers gathered around the fire engine. It was true that I'd wanted to attract attention to my new shop today, but this really wasn't what I'd had in mind.

Over the last few months, in my dreams, I'd pictured the people of this lovely town admiring my carefully designed window display, before rushing in to spend lots of money. Of course, in my nightmares, I'd seen the same people completely ignore my little shop.

I'd just spent all my savings, not to mention my borrowings, paying the decorators, shopfitters and suppliers, so it was natural that I was worried. What if nobody came into the shop? What if nobody wanted to order any flowers or buy any plants? I'd also stocked up on silk flowers and other accessories, and I'd spent hours over the last few days arranging and rearranging them on my displays.

I'd spent weeks swinging between over-the-top excitement at the thought of running my own business, and panic-stricken paranoia at the thought of going bankrupt. But, even in my worst moments, I'd never imagined my shop being flooded before I'd sold my first carnation.

'Park Street has a similar drain problem,' the fireman continued. 'The downpour was so sudden and ferocious, that it flooded a whole row of houses at six o'clock this morning.'

Great. Now he was trying to make me feel guilty as well. Of course, I knew having a home wrecked was worse than a shop and, logically, that should put my problems into perspective. But the size of my bank loan seemed to prevent me from feeling anything other than sick.

I stared at the "Opening Today" sign I'd stuck on the window late last night. I'd spent hours making the thing. Now it was just a blob of condensation-soaked paper. How much was all this going to cost me to put right? A fortune, no doubt.

'You are lucky you have a concrete floor, and your insurance should pay for any electrical repair work you need,' the fireman said, still trying to make me feel better. Then he stopped and asked, 'You are insured, I suppose?'

'Oh yes, I've paid extortionate insurance premiums,' I replied, trying not to think about how much extra they'd charge next year after this claim, assuming I still had a business by then.

'At least you're covered, that's the main thing,' he said before wading back into my shop.

Was it? Suddenly I felt terribly alone. It must be great to have someone special to turn to at moments like these, but the only person I could rely on was me. Which was why five months ago, after I'd been made redundant for the second time in two years, I'd decided to turn my flower arranging hobby into a profession and be my own boss. The job market on the Isle of Wight was limited, so why not give it a go. Which was why I'd put all my hopes and dreams into this shop. Now I had to make it work.

'Hi Fran, I only heard about this twenty minutes ago, and I got here as quickly as I could.'

I turned to see Carol rushing towards me. My heart soared as I looked at her smiling face. This was just what I needed, a friend to give me some moral support.

'Isn't this brilliant,' she added, shielding her camera from the rain.

'What do you mean, brilliant?' For heaven's sake, didn't anyone around here do sympathy?

'Sorry, I know it'll be a pain putting it right, but just think of the publicity I can get you,' she said, waving her press card at me. 'With any luck, I'll make you and your shop front page news on Friday.'

Half of me wanted to hit her but, even in my stressed state, I was impressed by her warped thinking. Front page of the local Isle of Wight paper, had to be better than the tiny advert I'd paid for on page twenty.

I watched in amazement as Carol went into bossy reporter mode and started ordering people about. She spoke to Brad – seems she knew all the firemen by name – and somehow persuaded him to make it look like he was carrying me out of the shop.

'It'll make a fantastic photo,' she said, as he scooped me up in his arms.

'You okay?' he asked, smiling at me. Which was when I noticed there was a good-looking guy beneath that helmet. I felt so safe with him holding me, that I almost gave up the struggle to be brave and let the tears come. Then Carol started shouting more orders, so I had to pull myself together again.

At around ten the rain finally stopped. I'd just finished talking to my insurance broker on my mobile when a lady stepped forward and asked, 'Are you Fran?'

I nodded.

'Oh dear,' she said. 'It does look a mess in there. I was told you were opening today, and I'd been hoping to see if you would do the flowers for my daughter's wedding. I do try and support local businesses where I can,' she explained. 'It's going to be in a marquee, and I was hoping you'd be able to do about twenty big displays of flowers as well as the normal bride and bridesmaid's bouquets. We've been talking about seven bridesmaids, but there might be a couple more.'

I just stared at her for a moment, then I started to smile for the first time that day.

'Don't worry about the shop not being open,' I said. 'I can call round to see you at your home any time to suit you and we can work out all the details. This is just a minor setback,' I said, waving a hand vaguely in the shop's direction.'

'Could you? That would be so good.'

Good! Was she joking? For an order that size I'd drive halfway up the country. Well, maybe not, but you know what I mean. After we'd made the appointment, several other people stopped to say how pleased they were that there was going to be a local florist back in the town.

"It's so nice to see you're going to be selling all the bits for my own flower displays,' one lady said, before explaining she did all the displays for the local church and was so glad to have somewhere just around the corner to purchase everything.

I promised her I'd be open tomorrow to let her buy whatever she needed regardless of the state of the shop.

'And if there's things you need that I don't have, I can always order it in for you.'

She seemed rather pleased, whereas I was ecstatic. I had customers.

I was allowed back inside around eleven-thirty. Most of the water had been pumped out but the carpet in the back room was still soaked. However, I was assured that a man and his super-sized vacuum was on his way to sort that. I tried not to think about how nice the carpet had looked yesterday. Instead, I dragged several rolls of ruined tissue paper out through the back door and dumped it in the bin. Then I set about seeing if anything could be salvaged from the waterlogged bottom drawer of the filing cabinet.

The hours zoomed past as I moved and cleaned and reordered things. I also rang my mother. You'd have though she of all people would be sympathetic, whereas in reality it was obvious she felt this whole problem would never have happened if only I had a man in my life.

'I really don't see how having a boyfriend would have changed anything,' I shouted down the phone. 'How many males do you know who can control the weather?'

She ignored this question, and started going on about my sister, and how happy she was now she had three children, two cats and a budgie.

'Mum, I'm in the middle of trying to sort things. I really don't have time for this now.'

'Fran dear, your priorities are all wrong,' she informed me.

'Probably,' I replied. 'But wrong or not, the electrician has just arrived and he's my top priority at the moment.'

He turned out to be a great guy but, as he was in his sixties and assured me he could do nothing about the weather, I decided not to make Mum's day and marry him.

During the afternoon it started raining again and, despite knowing it had been fixed, I ran outside to look at the drain. It seemed okay, but that didn't stop me panicking an hour later when my philosophical fireman walked in.

'I've come to get you out of here,' he said.

The fact he wasn't in uniform, made it seem all the more urgent and I started looking for signs of gushing water. At the thought of it all happening again, the room started to spin. Brad was by my side in an instant.

'I bet you haven't eaten today,' he said.

What did food have to do with anything? Didn't he realise I had more important things to concentrate on.

'I'll have to get the dehumidifier off the floor,' I cried. 'It's only hired, and they'll probably charge me if I let it drown.'

'Calm down, nothing's drowning,' Brad assured me. 'But you're likely to pass out if you don't stop and eat something soon. Carol said you'd do this, which is why I'm taking you to the café across the road.'

It took a while for me to understand Brad wasn't here in any official capacity and that I wasn't about to be flooded again. However, it was only after I'd checked to make sure the drain wasn't overflowing that I allowed him, for the second time that day, to guide me away from my precious shop.

I only realised how hungry I was as I started to eat the sausage sandwich he'd bought me. I'd been too nervous for breakfast, and since I'd arrived at work and discovered the water, I'd not even given food a thought. Now, as the tea warmed me, I started to relax.

Brad was telling me about life as a fireman, which was fascinating, but I couldn't help wondering why he was here with me.

'Did Carol put you up to this?' I asked, knowing my meddlesome reporter friend was more than capable of sticking her nose in where it wasn't wanted.

'Not exactly, but she did encourage me when I mentioned how much I liked you.'

He liked me? Suddenly I stopped focusing purely on my problems, and started noticing his blue eyes and that rather sexy stubbled chin.

We sat and talked for a while longer, then we went back to the shop and Brad helped me move a cabinet. I went to start to refill it, but he stopped me.

'Fran, leave it until tomorrow, you're exhausted,' he said softly. 'It's been a long day, and I think I should drive you home.'

That was an offer I couldn't refuse, so I emptied the dehumidifier and took a last look around. The walls would need repainting, the carpet would need replacing, but the flowers and plants, and most of my displays had somehow survived. I just needed to get rid of the terrible smell now.

But, on the plus side, I did have a few customers, and I was going to be front-page news. So, was Brad right about the flood being a golden opportunity?

Not a chance! To me it was still a major headache. Yet, as he held my hand and we walked towards his car, I had a feeling this day was going to end way better than it had started.

Nauseatingly Nautical

By the time Jack had pulled the dinghy ashore, I was feeling terrible. I'd assumed once I was back on dry land my stomach would stop churning, but it hadn't. My legs felt weak and floppy, like they were made of foam, and my head was pounding.

'Wasn't that fantastic?' Jack cried. 'See, Lizzy, I told you you'd love sailing. So how about doing the race with me next weekend?'

I tried to focus on his face. How could I tell him I'd hated every moment without it wrecking my chances with him?

'I'm not sure…' I started. I'd have said more, but I was too busy throwing up.

When Jack had first invited me sailing, I'd had romantic visions of a sun-drenched deck with me in a cute little bikini holding a glass of champagne. Which I suppose was daft considering Jack worked for the same firm I did, so he was hardly likely to be a millionaire.

He was, however, full of enthusiasm, so even when I discovered all he had was a dinghy I decided to give it a go. Mistakenly, I'd assumed it was some sort of engine driven inflatable. Not quite the sunbathing while sipping cocktails type of boat, more a sitting comfortably with a beer and the wind in your hair type. Which only proved I was raised in a concrete city and knew nothing about things nautical.

I wasn't even sure that Jack asking me to sail constituted a date, but I was living in hopes. He was good looking, friendly, just two years older than me and single. What wasn't to like? Except maybe his obsession with sailing.

My job had brought me to the Isle of Wight seven months ago. A place renowned for sailing, although so far Jack was the only person I'd met who actually went out on a boat, if you don't count the Island's ferries.

I didn't know a soul when I arrived here and, because I was working long hours, I'd not really met anyone apart from work colleagues, and most of them were married and had busy home lives. So how could I refuse Jack's invitation? When you're incredibly lonely you don't turn anything down, including sailing.

Nauseatingly Nautical

For our first boat trip, I'd carefully dressed in jeans and a strappy top and hoped I looked both seaworthy and sexy. I also packed a small picnic for us. How naïve could you get?

The first thing Jack did when I arrived at the sailing club was hand me a wetsuit.

'It was my sister's,' he said. 'But she only wore it twice, it should fit.'

I looked in horror at this weird rubbery contraption which nobody over the age of ten could possibly squeeze into. Then I noticed everyone was wearing such things, so I reluctantly took it into the changing room. After a lot of puffing, panting and several rude words, I forced my flesh into this thick blue second skin. The wetsuit emphasised every tiny bulge, and I was sure nothing other than a whale would find me attractive. Feeling very self-conscious, I picked up my food-laden bag and went to find Jack.

'Can't take anything with you,' he informed me. 'You'll lose it overboard with the first wave.'

I couldn't say I was worried about leaving the food behind because I'd rather lost my appetite, but surely Jack didn't expect me to go

Nauseatingly Nautical

out there without my handbag. No tissues, no hairbrush, no mobile phone? I felt so vulnerable. Naked almost.

It was while I was trying to digest this awful information that Jack showed me his dinghy. It was nothing like I'd expected. For a start it was really small, and didn't a boat need sides to stop it sinking? This thing looked more like a slightly bevelled board, it didn't have a back, or an engine, but it did have a frightening number of ropes.

Despite the warm weather, the sea felt icy as I stepped in and helped Jack launch.

'Don't worry,' he said, as he dragged me on board. 'With such light winds I'll be able to handle most things. You just enjoy yourself.'

Now that didn't sound too bad. Not that there was anywhere comfortable to sit, and the slightest ripple made the boat bounce. The water was just a few inches away, but it was fascinating watching the sails fill with wind as the boat started to move. Suddenly Jack yelled, 'Get ready.' Before I had time to ask, *'ready for what?'* he added, 'Let's go.'

It all happened very quickly. First, the sail swung towards me and only survival instinct made me duck in time. I started to fall backwards and screamed, which was when I discovered it isn't a good idea to hit the sea with your mouth wide open.

By the time I surfaced, the boat was floating upside down and Jack was standing on its bottom laughing. He got the boat upright easily. Getting me back on board took a bit longer.

'You'll have to learn to move quicker than that when we tack,' he said cheerfully. 'This boat isn't very forgiving.'

Humph, neither was I. I flicked my dripping wet hair back from my face and shuddered to think what my make-up must look like. I was also shivering as I happened to be very, very cold.

An hour later, and Jack had taught me to hurl myself under the boom when ordered, and I'd learnt to pull on a sheet. For some stupid reason, on a boat, a sheet was a rope. I had no idea what they put on beds, assuming you were luckily enough to be on a boat that was big enough to have a bedroom. Jack also showed me how my weight balanced the boat, and how it unbalanced it even faster. Six times I was thrown into the water, was it any surprise that I was sick?

'Don't worry,' Jack said, when I finally stopped being ill. 'Your system will adjust. You'll have your sea legs in no time.'

I didn't want sea legs. In fact, I wasn't sure I wanted to see the sea ever again. But after I'd somehow managed to claw my way out of my claustrophobic wetsuit, Jack took me into the clubhouse. He had a beer while I sat and sipped a glass of water, being as I couldn't face anything else.

Jack started telling me about how wonderful it felt to fly over the waves.

'It's such an exhilarating feeling when the wind is right and you're at one with the boat. Lizzy, I promise you, a couple more lessons and we can start racing seriously.'

As I said, Jack was so enthusiastic that it was easy to forget the last excruciating ninety minutes. Besides, I had nothing in my diary for the next four months except a trip home to see my parents, so surely learning to sail had to be better than being alone every weekend.

Before my next epic adventure, I nipped into the chemist. It was just three doors from my office, and this helpful man recommended some seasickness pills. I think they helped because that time I didn't disgrace myself. Plus, I only caused the boat to topple over on three occasions, so I was obviously improving.

The worst thing about that trip was the blisters on my hands from holding the... I'm sorry, I don't care if they do call them sheets, painters or halyards in the "Sailing Made Easy" book I was reading - the thing that rubbed away my skin was definitely a rope.

'Don't worry, it won't take long for your hands to harden up,' Jack promised, as if coarse hands were something that all twenty-seven-year-olds aimed for in life. And perhaps it was in his world because, so far, the only thing he'd ever really talked to me about was sailing. I was his crew, and I was beginning to wonder if he'd even noticed I was female.

Before work the next morning, I hobbled back into the chemists. This time the friendly guy recommended some cream for my blisters, and a spray for my poor aching muscles.

A few days later, Jack suggested we sail after work as well as at weekends. I was tempted to refuse, but what was the alternative? More lonely evenings in my poky flat watching reality telly?

It took a couple more lessons and another packet of seasickness pills before things on the boat started making sense. That did help, only I still wasn't quick enough when we tacked, and I kept being dumped in the sea with monotonous regularity.

In an effort to feel better about it all, and to maybe get Jack to notice that I wasn't just one of the guys, I decided to give up on the borrowed wetsuit and splash out on a cute, lightweight sleeveless one. In it I almost felt attractive.

The next day I didn't sneak out of the changing room, I walked out with my head held high. Jack looked at me, but his reaction wasn't the one I'd been hoping for.

'Oh dear, Lizzy, you'll regret that,' he said.

By the end of the race, I had to admit that Jack had a point about my new wetsuit. Without all that extra padding, sailing stopped being merely uncomfortable and was now extremely painful.

After all the weeks of suffering, I was now on first name terms with my friendly chemist.

Nauseatingly Nautical

'I'd recommend Arnica for those,' Andy suggested the next morning when I showed him the huge purple bruises on my legs and arms. I bought some more painkillers too and another lot of seasickness pills. Boy, was this sailing lark expensive!

Three days later I was supposed to go sailing again, and was so pleased when I woke up, looked outside and saw the lousy weather.

'What do you mean the race is still on,' I cried, when Jack rang and gave me the bad news.

'Well yes, I suppose I do get wet anyway, but what about all that wind?'

It seemed his boat loved these weather conditions and Jack felt that, for the first time, we really had a chance of doing well in the race. Suddenly spending a Sunday on my own seemed a wonderful idea. My relationship with Jack was going nowhere, and on my list of enjoyable pastimes sailing rated somewhere below a root canal at the dentist.

Of course, I was grateful to Jack for getting me out of my flat and introducing me to new people, and he'd always been so nice to me. Even if nice wasn't exactly what I was looking for in a man. Anyway, I didn't want to let him down. I took a double dose of seasickness pills, grabbed my well-padded wetsuit and decided today's race would be my last.

As I walked out of the changing rooms and took a proper look at the sea, I knew my decision to sail today was a big mistake. The waves were enormous and the sky ominously dark.

'You'll love it out there,' Jack promised when I voiced my concerns. 'This is what sailing is all about.'

I looked around and saw everyone else was climbing into their boats. Who wants to look a wimp? So, I gritted my teeth and went about helping Jack to launch the boat. That was a lot harder than usual, but Jack was right, once we were underway the speed was incredible.

And I didn't have a problem while we were going in a straight line, but at the first mark disaster struck. Well, to be more accurate the boom struck. It smacked me around the head. The last thing I remembered was putting my hand out to save myself.

Next thing I knew I was ashore, where I promptly ended my brief sailing career the same way I started it – by throwing up!

I spent a night in hospital with concussion, before returning home with two broken fingers and a black eye.

The following day I made a huge effort and got myself to work, where I was delighted to find heaps of tea and sympathy. At lunchtime, I went out to buy more painkillers.

'What on earth have you been up to this time?' Andy asked, rushing round the counter to take a closer look. He seemed very concerned as he inspected the ugly bump on my head.

'No, don't tell me, you went sailing again. Lizzy, it's none of my business, but are you sure you're cut out for such an energetic sport?'

'Don't worry, I've come to the same conclusion. I've told Jack to find himself another crew. Anyway, I can't do much for the next few weeks,' I said, holding up my poor broken fingers.

Andy inspected them for a few minutes.

'Do you know what I'd recommend for these?' he said.

'No doubt it'll be something really expensive and horribly smelly,' I replied.

He laughed.

Nauseatingly Nautical

'Well, sort of. I was thinking you look in need of some pampering. How about I treat you to a slap-up meal at our local Italian restaurant?'

'You serious?' I asked.

He nodded.

Well, what could I say but yes?

The next evening was brilliant. Andy was wonderful company, and I didn't get cold or wet or bruised. What more could a girl ask for?

For our second date, Andy took me to the cinema where we sat in the warm and dry, eating popcorn. It was heaven.

At the weekend, we went for a lovely walk along the beach. The waves lapped at our feet, and we both agreed this was the best way to experience the sea.

Isn't it funny how life's most awful experiences can sometimes end up bringing the most joy. If I hadn't gone sailing, I would never have discovered just how many ailments my clever chemist could cure. Especially that acute bout of loneliness I had. Andy has made sure I've recovered from that problem completely.

You Can't Have It All

Tara watched as two dogs played amongst the waves on the beach. For once, the sight didn't delight her. Even the sounds of the seagulls and the bright morning sunshine pouring through her cottage window only made her feel worse. Slowly she wandered into the kitchen. She couldn't face any breakfast but, with some effort, she did manage to make herself a coffee.

Taking the mug to the old oak table, she sat down and stared at the diamond ring sparkling on her finger. It was so beautiful and so new. She slipped it off her finger and laid it on the table. Had their engagement party only been last night? Was there a record for the shortest engagement? As yet more tears started to fall, she wondered if Euan had deliberately misled her. Perhaps it was her fault. Perhaps she was simply too obsessed with this cottage. Certainly her old boyfriend had thought so.

'I'm sorry Tara,' Alistair had shouted two years ago. 'I just don't see the attraction of some poky old cottage on the Isle of Wight. It hardly suits our lifestyle, does it!'

What he meant was that it didn't suit *his* lifestyle.

'But it would make a wonderful weekend home,' she'd argued.

'Do you really think you can afford to keep a weekend home?' he'd asked. 'On your wages?'

'The cottage was the only place I felt I belonged when I was growing up. The only place I was ever happy,' she'd tried to explain. She wanted him to understand.

'Tara,' he'd said firmly. 'I'm sure when your grandmother left you her cottage, she expected you to sell it.'

'I won't sell it,' she'd said. 'Don't you understand, it means too much to me.' But she could tell by the way he looked at her, he'd never understand.

'Your trouble is you want it all,' he shouted. 'And you can't have it all. No one can.'

These heated discussions continued for several months, until it became obvious she had to decide between Alastair and the cottage. He was right, she couldn't have it all. So, much to everyone's amazement, including her own, she packed in her job, said goodbye to Alastair, loaded up her car and drove down to catch the ferry to the Isle of Wight. She was eager to start her new life in the only place that had ever felt like home.

It was raining and almost dark when Tara had arrived at the cottage that first night. She'd been shocked to see how much the place had deteriorated in the seven months since her gran had died. It was cold, damp and smelly. She couldn't find how to switch on the main power for the lights, but she did find water dripping through the ceiling in one of the bedrooms.

Feeling very distressed, she went into the kitchen to see if she could light the old Aga. She was just beginning to realise she hadn't a clue how to do that, as it had never been turned off when Gran was alive, when the back door flew open.

'Don't move. I've called the police,' a deep male voice boomed at her. Then he fumbled with something in the back porch, and suddenly all the lights came on.

Standing in front of her, Tara saw a tall, strangely familiar looking man, waving an umbrella above his head.

'Euan, put that thing down. Can't you see you're scaring the poor girl,' said Mrs Duffy as she pushed past him. 'Oh, Tara, sweetie. Why didn't you let us know you were coming? We thought you were a burglar.'

'Hello, Mrs Duffy,' Tara said to her gran's neighbour. 'Am I glad to see you!'

Looking back at the man she grinned.

'I'd never have recognised you Euan.'

He gave her an embarrassed smile, as he tried to hide the umbrella behind his back.

'You've changed a bit too,' he muttered.

'Of course she's changed,' Mrs Duffy shouted impatiently at her son. 'She was only fifteen the last time you saw her.'

Tara soon found herself being bundled next door where, over a strong cup of tea, she explained her plans.

'That's wonderful,' said Mrs Duffy with a grin. 'This village needs more young beauties around the place. Now you must stay for something to eat.'

'That's very kind of you, Mrs Duffy, but I couldn't put you to all that trouble.'

'Oh, please call me Annie. And it's no trouble at all.'

Tara started to protest.

'If you're really going to live next door to my mother, you'd better understand there's no point in arguing with her. She'll get her own way. She always does,' Euan whispered to her,

Over a delicious dinner, Tara listened as Annie listed some of the problems with her cottage.

'It's going to need a fair bit spending on it,' Annie explained. Seeing Tara's worried look, she smiled encouragingly. 'Still, Euan comes to visit me most weekends, he can give you a hand.'

'I'm sure I can manage,' Tara said, with much more conviction that she felt.

After Euan went home, Annie insisted that Tara sleep in his old room.

'The bed next door will be far too damp,' she told Tara, who by this time was too tired to argue.

The next morning Tara went to her cottage to assess the problems. She was pleased to have Annie's moral support as she walked from room to room.

'Oh, you poor thing. You'll never manage all this on your own,' said Annie truthfully.

Tara thought about the small amount of money in her bank account and sighed. Then walking to the living room window, she opened it. She could hear the cries of the seagulls and watched as two fishing boats entered the harbour. But it was the salty sea breeze that convinced her she was home. And it was going to take more than a few holes in the roof and the odd bit of rotten wood to make her leave again.

Over the next few weeks Tara scrubbed and polished. and Annie helped when she could, which was lovely. Her habit of just walking into Tara's cottage unannounced took some getting used to, but Tara figured it was a lot better than the multiple mortise-locks she'd needed in place to feel safe in her flat in the city.

Annie, Tara soon discovered, was a born organiser. She organised a friend of hers to make the necessary repairs to the roof. She organised Euan to help Tara paint the water-stained walls. She also organised her poor son to move some of the larger pieces of furniture, to cut back the overgrown garden and repair the fence. Tara noticed he didn't seem to object, but maybe Annie had organised that as well.

But for all her abilities, even she couldn't organise a job for Tara. Despite her excellent PA skills, Tara was unable to find employment. Her money was disappearing fast, and the list of to-do jobs grew daily. As soon as she thought she'd fixed one problem, something else dropped off.

Then, on a crisp April day, her drains collapsed. Surrounded by estimates, bills and bank statements, she knew her dream was nearly over. Sobbing loudly, she didn't hear Euan come in.

'Mum's sent me round to look at…' he started, before rushing to her side. Then tissues and a mug of coffee seemed to appear from nowhere.

'I'm sorry,' she sniffed. 'I guess you must think I'm pretty silly getting so upset over a cottage.' She noticed he didn't disagree. 'My father died when I was three and mum remarried two years later,' she explained. 'I didn't get on with my stepfather, so I was sent here to stay with Gran whenever possible. I wanted to stay with her permanently, but I was too scared to ask. A pity because, just before she died, Gran admitted that she would have loved to have me live with her full-time. My childhood could have been so much happier.'

'I can remember watching you playing with a big doll in the garden,' Euan told her.

'I remember you always glaring at me over the fence.'

'Well, I thought you were just a silly little girl,' Euan laughed. 'But I was young, I hope I've changed a bit.'

And, just to prove how much, he took her out for a pub lunch. Tara enjoyed the break, it was nice to sit and listen to someone else's problems for a change. Euan was telling her about his work, and how unbelievably bad tempered his boss had become over the last week, since his P.A. had suddenly run off with the manager of their accounts department.

According to Euan the place was in chaos. Tara smiled sympathetically and said nothing.

The following morning, she got up early, dressed in her smartest suit and was sitting in reception when Euan's boss arrived.

'I'm the answer to all your problems,' Tara said as an introduction, and prayed very hard he wouldn't laugh in her face and throw her out.

He didn't. Impressed with her qualifications and determination, by ten o'clock he'd given her the job and a twenty-page report to type.

With a regular wage coming in, Tara was soon able to secure a small loan and employ someone to sort the drains. She was also able to get the electrics upgraded and buy some new radiators that actually heated up in the cold weather.

She still had loads of plans for the place, but they would have to wait a while. In the meantime, she was enjoying her first summer alone in her cottage. She'd get up early in the morning and stroll along the beach before work. It was paradise.

Seeing Euan every day was also something she was starting to enjoy. He was out working on-site a lot of the time, so the contact was mainly five minutes in the mornings, but it was nice to start the day with a friendly face. Not that she wasn't enjoying the job, and her new boss seemed happy with her.

Annie was still organising Euan to help at the cottage at weekends. Tara had told him numerous times that he didn't need to do it, but he seemed to enjoy coming over and helping her, and she certainly appreciated it.

Together they decorated the outside of the cottage. He did all the high stuff on the ladder as she wasn't good with heights. He also helped with decorating the stairs for the same reason.

He was fun to have around and by the end of the summer, Tara was feeling very contented with her life.

It was strange in some ways that she didn't realise she was in love with Euan until the following Christmas. And then it was Annie, and her conveniently placed mistletoe, that instigated their first kiss. Euan was the most wonderful, caring, considerate man she had ever met. So, last week when he'd asked her to marry him, she'd had no hesitation in saying yes.

Annie was so thrilled she'd organised a big engagement party. Almost all the village turned up. Tara was delighted. She had good friends, the man she loved, a home she adored, and a great job. What more could a girl want? Alastair, her ex-boyfriend, had been wrong. She could have it all.

Tara sat sobbing at the kitchen table. Her coffee had gone cold, and she knew how it felt. She'd been so happy as Euan had walked her home after the party last night.

'I love you Euan Duffy,' she'd told him, as they'd walked up to her front door. 'And I promise I'm going to make you a wonderful wife.'

'Of course you are,' he agreed. 'You're going to look after me just like mum used to.'

'Well,' she laughed. 'I can't promise to cook as well as her. I think we may have to get rid of the Aga and replace it with a microwave.'

'I assure you we won't have an Aga in our new home.'

She stopped laughing.

'What new home?'

'Whatever one we choose,' he said.

'I'm not leaving my cottage.'

'Tara,' he said, trying to take her in his arms. 'I know the cottage means a lot to you. But as much as I love her, I'm sorry, I can't live next door to Mum.'

Tara couldn't believe it. All this time they'd spent together, all the time they'd talked about their future, never once had Euan mentioned this. She'd never mentioned it either, because she'd assumed he understood how much the cottage meant to her. Their row had been short, but fierce.

So here she was once again faced with a choice - the cottage or the man. She'd fought so hard for this place, and she still had so many plans for it. She couldn't give it up now.

She'd cried the whole night. Leaving Alastair had been difficult, but also a relief in an odd sort of way, yet the thought of losing Euan terrified her.

Hearing a noise behind her, Tara turned and found Annie standing in the doorway.

'Euan's in my place,' she said. 'He's very upset.'

Tara didn't answer.

Annie threw away the cold coffee and made them a pot of tea.

'Euan's explained the problem,' she said quietly. 'It's nice to know you'd be happy living next door to me. But he's right, it wouldn't work. I'd interfere far too much. And I'm going to interfere again,' she said with a smile. 'I've got my eye on those lovely retirement homes over the way.'

Tara looked horrified.

'You can't move into a retirement home,' she gasped. 'You are way too young. And you love your garden. No Annie, it's a crazy idea.'

'Of course I'm too young,' agreed Annie. 'At least, I am at present. But I made up my mind when they first built the place, that one day I'm going to move there. It'll be perfect for when I get too old to manage the garden and stairs. And, Tara sweetie, in the meantime I know someone who'd just love to rent this cottage of yours.'

Tara felt her heart skip a beat, and her mind started to race. Rent out the cottage? Would it be possible to rent out her beloved cottage now, and then return to it at some future time when the situation had changed?

Annie leaned over and patted Tara's hand.

'In case you're wondering, Euan thinks it's a great idea. Even if it came from his interfering old mum. You know lass,' Annie continued. 'You can't have it all, but if you look hard enough, you can find a pretty good compromise.' After a long pause, she added. 'But Euan doesn't believe you love him enough to compromise over this cottage.'

'Then Euan's wrong,' Tara said jumping up. 'I love him too much to lose him.' And, with more tears pouring down her face, she leaned over and gave Annie a big hug. 'I think you're going to make a terrific mother-in-law.'

'Of course. It's what I always intended to be,' Annie muttered quietly, as she watched Tara rush across the garden and fall into her son's waiting arms.

The End of an Era

Doug spent ages wandering around the bleak, empty shop, which looked much smaller now it was devoid of stock. It was hard to leave, but he'd swept it out twice, taken the final meter readings four times and now there wasn't anything left to do except cry. And he was determined that he wasn't going to do that. At least, not here. So, with a twisted feeling in the pit of his stomach, he took his keys and slowly locked the front door for the very last time.

He still couldn't believe it had come to this. For thirty years he'd run his little hardware store and, whilst it hadn't made him a fortune, he'd enjoyed every minute of it. By knowing his customers he'd survived the opening of a massive DIY superstore twenty years ago, but he couldn't fight on-line shopping.

He still had his loyal customers, but he hardly saw anyone new these days. Since lockdown he'd watched three of his neighbours shut up shop and another go bust. Plus three multinational stores had closed their doors in this town. His end of the High Street was just a mass of empty shops, so no one really had any reason to come to this part of town any longer. It didn't take a genius to work out that if he didn't close the business soon, he'd end up going bust as well.

Helen, his wife, kept telling him they were lucky coming out with their savings intact, and he knew she was right. But no matter how hard he tried, Doug didn't feel lucky.

As he posted the shop keys thorough the landlord's door, he thought about the day he'd picked up those very same keys. Helen had been so encouraging when he'd first seen the shop and said he'd like to run his own business. She'd been happy for him to take the risk, and he'd been both excited and terrified. Now he was just scared of the empty days stretching out in front of him.

Perhaps he'd been stupid, but he'd always imagined he'd still be running the shop at eighty. At sixty-four, he'd never given retirement a thought. What was he going to do with the rest of his life?

The End of an Era

Doug drove home the long way, going as slowly as he could. He wanted to put off the inevitable moment when he'd arrive home and could let all his emotions out. But finally he had to face it, and as he pulled onto the drive Helen came rushing out the house and stood by the car. He really wasn't sure he could cope with tea and sympathy.

'Where have you been?' she shouted. 'You should have been home ages ago. We've only got half an hour before we have to leave. I'll load the suitcases in the car while you go and change.' With that, she took the car keys and dashed back to the house.

He was still standing by the car feeling totally confused when she came out lugging the first suitcase. Being a gentleman, he hurried over and took it from her.

'What's going on?'

'Haven't time for explanations,' Helen replied, glancing at her watch. 'Let's just say this is the start of our new life, and you're already running late for it.'

When he didn't move, Helen gave him a quick kiss.

'I promise I'll explain it all in the car darling, but for now please put down the case and go and get changed – quickly!'

As Doug took a fast shower, he decided tea and sympathy might have been preferrable after all.

With dripping hair, he climbed into the car as his wife revved the engine and reversed off the drive very fast. Unlike him, Helen did everything in top gear, she always had done. It was one of the things Doug loved about her.

'As long as we don't hit heavy traffic, we should still make it,' Helen stated.

Doug assumed she'd planned all this to stop him coming home from the shop and falling to pieces. However, this was the end of an era, and he felt he could easily fall to pieces wherever he was.

When they turned onto the motorway, Doug finally asked where they were going.

'You are never going to guess,' she said with a laugh.

Doug decided if she thought he wasn't going to guess then there was no point trying. So he just sat there glumly looking at the car in front.

'I can give you a clue,' Helen added. 'I thought we'd go back to where it all began forty years ago.'

He turned and looked at her.

'We're going to the Isle of Wight?'

'Spot on,' she laughed. 'And guess where we're staying.' She paused a bit before continuing. 'I've booked us a place where you used to live on Gurnard Marsh.'

Good grief, had she gone mad? He used to rent a tatty old shack there, why on earth would she want to go back to something like that.

Back when he was twenty-one, Doug had felt he was the luckiest guy in the world when he'd landed a job teaching youngsters to sail. Since the age of eight he'd loved being on the water, and being able to move to Cowes and sail every day was a dream come true. Especially as they were paying him to do it.

Finding affordable accommodation wasn't so easy, which was how he'd ended up living in an old wooden shack on the Marsh. The rent had been cheap, which almost made up for the fact that there were so many gaps in the wood that the wind managed to find places to howl through, regardless of which direction it was blowing. And when it rained it sounded like a sledgehammer was hitting the corrugated roof.

He had running hot water, but only from a tiny wall heater. Luckily, he was able to shower at work.

When he mentioned this to Helen, she simply laughed.

'Doug, that was forty years ago, you don't really think those old shacks are still there. I've booked us into a chalet.'

Ah, they had chalets on the Marsh back then too, some of them in a worse condition than the shack.

'I can assure you the chalet has a fully functioning bathroom,' she said.

That's as maybe, Doug thought, but he bet it was still noisy when it rained, and judging by those clouds it was about to do just that. He slunk lower in his car seat and wished he were home where he could sneak off to his shed and mope in peace. He felt empty and old, and revisiting his youthful past was the last thing he needed.

As he sat and watched the miles go by, Doug remembered the day he met Helen. It was August

1984, and the sailing conditions were perfect. Whenever work gave him the choice, he'd opt to take the younger kids out on the water and teach them to sail. He had no problems laughing and joking with ten-year-olds, whereas twenty-year-old girls tended to make him blush a lot.

That day he got lucky, he was assigned Helen. He may not have been that happy to start with, but he soon discovered this girl was different. She was staying with friends in Cowes for the summer, and he immediately felt at ease with her.

She'd fearlessly jumped into the little dinghy, even though she knew nothing. She'd laughed when she capsized the boat and was thrown headfirst into the Solent. They soon discovered she was hopeless at sailing, but that didn't stop her enjoyment.

She completely captivated him and, despite his shyness, he managed to ask her to join him on a walk one evening. He was amazed and delighted when she'd said yes.

After that, they spent every free moment together. By the end of her holiday they were in love. Doug asked her to stay with him on the Island, but he understood why she said no.

The End of an Era

Unlike him she had a loving family, and she wanted to stay close to them. So, he threw in his job, moved to the Midlands and they married ten months later. He'd never once regretted it.

'The car ferry's better these days,' Helen commented an hour later, as they drank coffee on the top deck.

'Most of the sailing boats look better too,' Doug replied, as he stood by the railings studying the many yachts on the Solent. It was years since he'd been sailing. He'd taken the children when they were very young, but since he'd started the business he hadn't had much free time.

Doug took over the driving when they returned to the car. It felt strange driving off the ferry after all these years. He wondered if he'd be able to remember his way around, after all he hadn't been back in over thirty-five years.

'This looks different but it's still noisy,' he commented, as the clunking chains on the East Cowes Floating Bridge pulled them across the River Medina.

Apart from several new blocks of flats, the seafront looked much as Doug remembered. And Gurnard Marsh hadn't changed that much either.

The End of an Era

It was still little more than a row of quaint holiday chalets and a boat park running parallel to the sea.

'That chalet hasn't changed a bit since my day,' Doug said, pointing to a very dilapidated building.

'But look, the rest have been upgraded,' Helen pointed out, and he had to admit she was right.

As Doug parked outside their chalet, even in his depressed state he was impressed by how smart it looked. Helen was out of the car in a flash and rushed to open the door. Inside was lovely. He wished he'd had something like this forty years ago. Even the bathroom was perfect he decided after he'd run the tap and found there was plenty of hot water.

After they'd unpacked, Helen opened a bottle of wine.

'Here's to our future,' she said, as they stood outside on the patio.

'I'd forgotten how spectacular the sunsets are from here,' Doug said, as they gazed at the breathtaking red streaked sky. For a moment he thought maybe this was helping, but then he remembered he'd just lost his business, and he found his eyes filling with tears.

Despite everything, Doug slept well that first night and Helen had to wake him the next morning.

'Come on sleepyhead,' she laughed. 'It's a sunny day, and I thought we could explore the area.'

'I'd like to take a look at Gurnard Sailing Club,' Doug replied, as he dragged himself out of bed.

'All I remember are those rickety old steps up to the club house,' Helen said. 'I should think the place has fallen into the sea by now.'

Walking to the sailing club was something Doug had done many times when he lived here. Teaching sailing in Cowes was his job, but racing his dinghy from Gurnard was pure pleasure, and that was how he'd spent all his free time. It was a shame he was too old for such things these days.

Most of the houses looked familiar on the walk, and he was pleased to see the big pub on the corner was still there, but the sailing club had changed completely. Where once a rickety old wooden building had stood, there was a bright white modern building,

'I think we'll see if we can have lunch at the pub later,' he said, but first he wanted to see what kind of dinghies the folks around here were sailing these days. Being a Sunday, the place was buzzing with sailors preparing for the morning race.

As Doug walked between the boats, he was amazed to see a face he knew. The two men stared at each other. The forty years since they'd last sailed together slipped away.

'Tim, I don't believe it,' Doug cried, staring at the man standing there in a wetsuit. 'Don't tell me you're still sailing dinghies.'

Actually, as Doug soon discovered, there were quite a few baby boomers in amongst the teenagers. Their hair, or what was left of it, might be grey, and there might be a few wrinkles he hadn't seen before, but he had no problem recognising them.

As he started to say hello, it felt like he'd only been away a few months.

'I'm short of a crew today,' one of the guys called out. 'How do you fancy coming out on the boat with me?'

Doug wasn't sure what to say, so he turned to look at Helen.

'Off you go,' she said, giving him a little push. 'I'll be happy sitting here drinking coffee and watching you.'

'Are you sure?' he asked, half wishing she'd said not to be so silly, and that at his age he needed to take it easy.

Less than an hour later the race started.

'You weren't hoping to win this were you?' Doug asked, as he helped haul the boat upright again. 'I don't think I'm as agile as I used to be.'

Luckily, by the end of the race, it was all coming back to him, so he didn't disgrace himself by making them come last.

'That was amazing,' Doug said, as he walked over to Helen.

'At first, I thought you were going to spend all your time with the boat upside down,' she laughed. 'But I see you improved.'

In the end they stayed and had lunch at the club. Doug still couldn't get over how many people he knew, but then why would anyone want to move away from such a beautiful location? He'd only left because he'd fallen in

The End of an Era

love with Helen. He glanced over at her, and saw she was happily chatting to a group of women.

'Do you want to crew for me again on Wednesday evening?' he was asked.

'I'd love to,' he replied. He didn't refuse an invitation to try out a catamaran on Tuesday afternoon either. Although, as his muscles started to remind him that he hadn't used them for a while, he did wonder if this was sensible.

By the end of their week, Doug had been sailing four times and every muscle ached. But instead of lying awake at night worrying, he'd slept soundly.

'It's been a wonderful holiday,' Doug said, as they packed the car. During the week they'd driven around the Island, and they'd been delighted to see it was still as pretty as ever. Their chalet had been cosy, and the area was much nicer for the pumping station that now stopped the constant flooding. But the highlight had been realising he wasn't too old to go dinghy sailing.

'I had a feeling this would do you good,' Helen said. Then they started to speak together.

'Helen, do you think we could afford to come over more often?'

The End of an Era

'Look Doug, the family's all grown and have moved away. We could easily sell up and move over here.'

'Did I hear you right?' Doug asked. 'Did you say you'd be happy to live here?'

'It's not only the chalets that have changed over the last forty years. Moving to the Island would be perfect for us.'

Doug threw his arms around his wife.

'Do you think we ought to let an estate agent look at the house to see how much it's worth.'

'That's a great idea, I can ring…'

Helen was in full swing as her fast-action brain started planning all the things they would need to do as soon as they reached home.

Doug smiled as he started driving to the ferry, why had he been so worried about losing the business. With a wonderful wife like Helen at his side, he should have known this wasn't the end of an era – it was simple the start of a new one.

In Need of Some First Aid

The moment I saw the blood my head started spinning, my skin went clammy, and I felt sick. Great, that's just the reaction you'd want from someone manning a first aid station. Now Liam was bound to wonder why I'd volunteered to help him today. Oh please, don't let him work out it was only because I fancied him.

Liam was busy clearing up the large amount of shattered glass and orange juice before anyone else could hurt themselves, so it wasn't until he turned around that he spotted I was having problems.

'You carry on there, I'm coping fine,' I lied, as I desperately tried to remember the procedure for dealing with deep cuts. Only it was no good, my brain wouldn't function with all that red stuff gushing everywhere.

Even though I was sitting down the floor suddenly started to get a little closer, and Liam only just caught me before I hit it.

'Come on Hannah,' he said, gently guiding me into the right position.

Having him so close should have been a dream come true, but it just made me feel worse. I was supposed to be helping him, not giving him extra problems. Not that he looked in the least fazed by any of it. He was staying amazingly calm, and he was wonderfully reassuring as he grabbed the first aid kit and took over attending the nasty cut.

I felt such an idiot as I kept still and tried to swallow my humiliation. Liam was every inch the professional, and I hated him seeing that I was a complete wimp.

The trouble was, on the first aid course I took seven months ago, they didn't use real blood. They didn't even use fake stuff. And, if I'm honest, I only took the course because our company needed an extra first aider on the books, and the lucky person got a pay increase. But I wasn't stupid, I did go and check to see what sort of accidents the first aiders had dealt with over the last three years. Seemingly there

In Need of Some First Aid

were only three "incidents" in the Accident Book. One was Lucy, when she needed a plaster for a small cut on her finger after she'd tried to free up a trapped chocolate bar from the vending machine. One was another plaster needed after a rather nasty paper cut. The third one was when one of the engineers who, despite working with large, complicated machinery all day, had managed to mess up using a tiny stapler and put a staple in his thumb. I reckoned even I could cope with those things, probably without getting any training.

The First Aid Course, however, had been very interesting and I'd passed it fine. But then it had been fairly basic, and I haven't needed the skills since. Well, not until now. Today was our firm's annual recruitment day. It was where the management opened our doors to several coach loads of university students.

Health and Safety rules meant we had to have first aid cover available, and last week I was asked if I'd like to spend the afternoon in the medical room with Liam. Well, what girl wouldn't?

Liam worked on the admin side of our engineering department, and I only saw him once a month when I went into his office to collect the timesheets. He was always friendly and chatty, and over the last few months I'd managed to discover that he wasn't married. Lucy, who seemed to know everything about everyone, said he wasn't seeing anyone but did admit that her info might be out of date.

It was hardly a subject I could bring up when I was only in his office for five minutes a month. However, I figured working alongside him in the First Aid Room for half a day would give me the chance to get to know him properly. You know, find out if my lusting from afar was just a waste of time or if I stood a chance.

Although, as lovely as the idea of working alongside Liam was, I did first check the sort of casualties we were likely to get. I discovered that last year they'd only had three students visit the medical room. One wanted change for the coffee machine, and the other two wanted directions to the toilets. Now that I could cope with.

I'd spent the last week hoping that, after spending some time alone with me, Liam would notice what a great person I was. We met up at midday and, until ten minutes ago, it had been going really well. Four hours and not a single person came anywhere near us.

I'd found out he'd just bought a flat, which he lived in on his own. There was no girlfriend, and he took his first aid very seriously. Weekends he worked with a firm who provided first aid cover for events across the Isle of Wight, which proved he was even nicer than I'd imagined. I felt so comfortable with him, or I had until this happened. Now I was sure he'd just see me as a useless waste of space. I was gutted.

'Has your head stopped spinning Hannah?' he asked.

'I think so,' I said, lifting it carefully. 'Look, I'm sorry about this, it's just I've never dealt with that much blood before.'

'Don't worry, it's something you get used to. Now, I've cleaned out all the glass and it's not bleeding anywhere near as much, so do you feel up to practising your skills by dressing the wound?'

Not really, but I wasn't going to admit that. After all, until a few minutes ago, Liam had been trying to persuade me to join the Island's first aid team. He'd been making me laugh with some of the dafter things that had happened at a local horse show recently, but he'd also been impressing me with the different type of events he helped cover. Local fetes, carnivals, concerts, sporting events.

'If there aren't many casualties, then we can get to see some of what is going on, but other times we're so busy we have no idea what's happening around us,' he'd said.

'What type of injuries do you deal with?' I'd asked.

'Everything. A lot of the summer events are in open fields, so there are bee stings, heat exhaustion and twisted ankles. I've even had to deal with the odd heart attack, which is very scary. But I saved two people's lives last year and that is so rewarding. I love my job here, but I also love the first aid work I do.'

Boy, had he done an excellent sales job on me. Until I saw all that blood, I'd been seriously thinking about joining. And no, it wasn't just because the idea of spending every weekend with Liam appealed so much, although that would be a bonus. I just liked the sound of going to these places and being useful. I was twenty-six years old, and my weekends normally consisted of shopping, clubbing and sleeping late. It was hardly a rewarding lifestyle.

'But I've only got a basic first aid certificate,' I'd reminded him.

'That's not a problem. If you're really interested, I can help you get the other qualifications,' he'd promised me.

Which meant seeing him evenings during the week as well, which was also appealing. Or it had been. Now look at me. But not wanting to look a total idiot, I took a deep breath, picked up the first aid box and went back to work.

'You've done that really well,' Liam said, after he'd inspected my dressing. 'I think you'd make a great first aider.'

He does?

'But what good is someone who's going to faint at the first injury?' I sighed.

He looked me in the eyes – which was bliss.

'Lots of doctors pass out the first time they see an operation taking place,' he said. 'That doesn't stop them going on to make excellent surgeons.' Then he grinned, 'Besides, Hannah, it's always worse when it's your own blood. Now, how's your foot feeling?'

In Need of Some First Aid

'It stings a lot, but I think I'll live. I can't believe the only casualty we've had all afternoon is me.'

'It could have been worse. It could have been me,' he laughed. 'Then what would we have done when you fainted?'

Liam helped me stand.

'I don't think you ought to drive, Hannah. So how about I take you home as we've finished up here. We could even stop for something to eat on the way, if you promise not to drop anything on your foot again.'

He slipped his arm around me as he helped me stand up. Suddenly I felt myself starting to sway again. Only no one needed a first aid certificate to work out what was causing my head to spin this time.

A Lack of Maternal Instinct

I think it must have been about 1980 when Karen and I were first asked what we wanted to be when we grew up. We'd been best friends since the first day we started school, and we must have been about eleven when faced with the question.

Karen had no hesitation in replying that she wanted to be a mummy and push her baby around the park all day. I remember looking at Karen in horror and declaring that babies were smelly, noisy things and I certainly didn't want one of those. I loved animals and had decided that I was going to be a vet.

We'd both been born on the Isle of Wight and, as we grew up, we spent a lot of our spare time either on Karen's family farm, or at the beach. Both ideal places to influence our outlook on life.

We both saw plenty of animals born on the farm, and I loved helping feed the baby lambs in the spring. At the beach we got to see a lot of small humans, they were mainly crying or shrieking too loudly.

In the fields I saw the cows and sheep gently nuzzling their young as they ambled around. All I saw on the beaches were frazzled looking parents trying to keep their little monsters under control.

At the age of eighteen, I gave up the idea of being a vet when I realised just how much yucky stuff the job entailed, and I settled on a more sensible career path – accountancy.

Off I went to one university, while Karen went off to a different one to study agriculture. She was going to end up running the family farm one day, and I could picture her in the future running around with a baby tucked under one arm and a piglet under the other. But whilst I'd changed my mind about my career, I hadn't changed my mind about motherhood. I never wanted a life of sleepless nights, dirty nappies and temper tantrums. I wanted a smart business suit, a sports car and a luxury apartment.

For a while I was afraid my friendship with Karen would fade as we went our separate ways, but it never did. Karen remained my best friend despite our many differences, or maybe it was because of them.

By the time I'd taken my last exam and finished my in-house training, Karen was back on the Isle of Wight and had met and married Stuart. They'd bought a little house close to the farm.

I even stayed with them a couple of nights when I came across to the Island for a job interview.

'I don't want to mention this to Mum in case I don't get it,' I told Karen, and then admitted the other two jobs I'd applied for were in Leeds and Nottingham.

'You can't live that far away from the Island,' she protested.

I agreed that it wasn't what I wanted either, but good jobs were hard to find.

As it was, I didn't get any of them, but I did eventually get a nice position with a small accounting firm in Southampton. Which meant I

A Lack of Maternal Instinct

could live with my parents and simply commute to work on the ferry each day. And I got to spend time with Karen and Stuart, and a few other old friends. It suited me just fine.

Two years later I bought my own place, it was as far from being a luxury apartment as you could get, but at least I had a foot on the property ladder. Karen was also on her way to making her dreams come true. She was pregnant.

Zoe was six hours old the first time I saw her.

'Isn't she the most beautiful baby you've ever seen?' Karen asked.

'Well, she's certainly the youngest,' I muttered tactfully, as I peered at a bundle of red wrinkles. Gas and air had obviously done something to my friend's eyesight, not to mention her memory, because the next thing Karen was dumping the baby in my arms. Me, the girl who'd always hated playing with dolls.

'Hey, Leah is looking all maternal, we must have a photo of this,' Karen said to her husband. I wasn't sure how she could have mistaken my terrified expression for one of motherly love, but she had been up all night, so perhaps she had an excuse.

'You'll be wanting one next,' Stuart laughed as he grabbed the camera.

Sorry, the only thing I wanted was to give the baby back before I dropped it, or it started crying, or it did something disgusting down my white blouse. I was there to make sure Karen had survived this terrible ordeal. I'd brought presents and was happy to coo at the baby with the same enthusiasm I showed when forced to look at other people's holiday snaps. But that was as far as I was prepared to go. Best friend or not, I had my limits.

The next three years were busy ones. I earned a nice promotion and bought a cheap pseudo sports car. I had my share of boyfriends, but they never lasted long because either they were unreliable jerks, or they wanted a permanent relationship that included settling down and starting to reproduce. Seriously, why were there no nice guys who also wanted to remain childless? Of course, I did meet the odd divorced guy who already had his 2.4 child quota, but I soon

A Lack of Maternal Instinct

discovered that I didn't have the required skills for step-parenting either.

Every time I saw Karen, it just reinforced my complete lack of maternal instincts. I had no idea why, but little children terrified me. Karen was a natural with Zoe, whereas I simply had no idea what to do. I preferred seeing Karen when her daughter was in bed, and I thought the biggest problem in my life was if I timed it wrong and ended up near Zoe and her little sticky fingers. Turned out that her sticky fingers were the least of our worries.

Karen rang me one afternoon in floods of tears. At first, I'd assumed it was her dad as he'd been in hospital several times over the previous month, but it wasn't. Stuart, her wonderful and loving husband, had been killed in a car crash. How could this happen? Nothing in life so far had prepared us for this.

With her dad being ill, Karen and her mum were already busy trying to run the farm short-handed. I did what any good friend would do, I tried to help. I provided a shoulder for Karen to cry on, which she did constantly. And I used my skills to sort out her finances, the endless paperwork and argue her case with the insurance company. This I could cope with because I had no problem with lawyers, bank managers or court officials, but leave me alone in a room with a hyperactive three-year-old and I turned into a gibbering idiot.

But it was impossible to ignore Zoe, the poor child had lost her father and her mother was heartbroken. Karen's aunt moved into the farmhouse to help her mum care for her dad, which meant Karen and Zoe were on their own in the cottage along the road.

The farm was hard work, and with everyone grieving and worrying about Karen's dad, I started visiting as much as I could.

Poor Karen was usually exhausted at the end of trying to survive another day, so I'd go straight from the ferry to see her. I'd make dinner and then put Zoe to bed, giving Karen a little time to herself.

I was amazed at how well I coped with getting Zoe into her nightclothes and reading a bedtime story or two. And after a while I found I wasn't just coping, I was enjoying it.

After a year, things settled into a routine as both Karen and her dad started to recover. Zoe was growing fast, and she looked adorable in her new school uniform.

Funny, but I never saw it happening. One day Zoe was simply a child I saw for Karen's sake, the next she'd stolen my heart. Maybe it happened when the little scamp was in bed and would put her chubby little arms around my neck and whisper, 'I love you Auntie Leah.'

Which I was sure was just a clever ploy to make me stay and read to her longer, but I would hold her in my arms and, just for a moment, I wouldn't want to let her go. It even made me question my childless future.

However, helping Karen with Zoe's birthday party cured me of that. Ten five-year-olds, a gooey chocolate cake and a thunderstorm that meant they'd all had to stay inside was a nightmare. After what felt like a lifetime, the children were collected, the clearing up was done and I staggered to my car. Give me a set of complicated accounts any day.

I was thirty-three when they made me a partner in the business. I was able to buy a place closer to the ferry, making my daily commute easier. I also started looking at nicer cars.

A Lack of Maternal Instinct

I loved my new role, but it brought new pressures which meant the couple of evenings each week I spent with Karen and Zoe were precious to me. With them I could forget the problems at work and simply play silly games with Zoe while chatting to my dearest friend.

I was so grateful to Karen for allowing me a tiny share of her daughter, especially as I only had the good bits. I got all the fun jobs like taking Zoe to the pantomime and spoiling her with new clothes, toys and sweets. Karen had to deal with the snotty noses, the stomach-aches and making her eat her greens. I couldn't have been happier with the arrangement.

Of course, there was always this nagging voice inside me that said I shouldn't get too attached to Zoe. When Karen married again, and I had no doubt one day she would, Zoe would have a whole new family. She'd hardly need someone like me in her life.

Not that I took my own advice. Over the next two years I saw more, not less of Zoe.

'Leah, are you sure you don't mind having Zoe for two nights? You know she never stops talking these days,' Karen said the first time she agreed to go up north and meet Craig's parents.

'If I can't cope I'll scream, and your new boyfriend will have to rush you back here. But I'm sure Zoe will be fine, so stop worrying.' I gave Karen a hug, and hoped she wouldn't sense how nervous I was about being responsible for a chattering ten-year-old. Although if push came to shove, I knew where Karen's mum lived. Karen's dad had never completely recovered, but they loved having Zoe visit. However, Karen thought a couple of days would be too much for them. I just hoped it wouldn't be too much for me too.

It was strange, but fifteen minutes after Karen had left, I stopped worrying. Zoe was so excited about staying with me that all my fears disappeared. We spent the afternoon walking along the seafront and playing in the park, before ending the day with a pyjama party. It was just like the ones I'd had with her mum at that age, and I wasn't sure which of us enjoyed it the most – probably me!

After that, Zoe regularly came to me while Karen spent time with Craig. And, just in case Zoe worked out that it was terribly uncool to be seen with a friend of her mum's, I bought myself my dream sports car with a push button retractable roof, guaranteed to impress any growing child. Overall, my whole life at that point was going pretty well. What could possibly go wrong?

'You want me to set up and run the new office?' I said at the next partner's meeting. We'd already expanded into Portsmouth, and I'd done a fair bit of the work getting that up and running, now we had the chance to take over an office in Reading. I was delighted they wanted me to organise it all, but with the Portsmouth office I'd still commuted daily. I couldn't do that working in Reading.

'For someone who doesn't like kids, you're getting awfully upset,' Seb, a friend at work, said three weeks later as I tearfully cleared my desk.

'Zoe isn't just any kid.'

'But it's not like you'll never see her again,' he pointed out.

'I won't see her as often, and it's not like I'm family or anything, she'll forget who I am.' I could tell Seb didn't understand, but he gave me a hug and muttered some reassuring words.

A Lack of Maternal Instinct

It was never easy explaining my relationship with Zoe, because even I wasn't sure what it was. I just knew she was very important to me, and now I was going to lose her. I knew I'd be too busy to come back many weekends, at least for the first six months. And even when I did, weekends were the time Karen and Zoe spent with Craig, and that relationship had to come first.

I really wanted the job in Reading, but I was afraid that losing Zoe was too high a price to pay. However, staying was daft because she was getting older, and I was sure that fairly soon she'd stop wanting to spend time with me anyway. Which was why I finally packed my bags, rented out my flat, and drove my lovely little car to Reading.

After the move, Karen and I talked on the phone several times a week and, much to my amazement, Zoe always wanted to chat to me too. In fact, sometimes I ended up talking to Zoe for longer than I did her mother. It was very odd, but I wasn't complaining.

A Lack of Maternal Instinct

Zoe was fourteen when things changed at work and I ended up back at the Southampton office. I was delighted, not that I hadn't loved my time in Reading, but it meant I could return to the Island. I could be closer to my folks as they were getting older, and I had really missed spending time with Karen, not to mention Zoe.

I'd now sold my old place, and this time I went out and bought an apartment overlooking the sea. This was the home I'd always dreamed I'd have. I didn't expect to see a lot of Zoe, but I hadn't reckoned on her liking the peace and quiet of my place. Something I shamelessly took advantage of.

As Zoe was in her exam years, she needed somewhere to do her homework. Karen had by now married Craig, and his twin boys often stayed with them. Her and Craig were planning on moving house, but for the time being it was a tight squeeze in her little cottage.

'I do love my new brothers, but they make such a noise and are into everything. Last week one of them smudged chocolate all over my history essay,' she said one evening as she settled at my computer to do her latest school project.

'They are only seven, they'll grow out of it. Maybe.' I laughed.

I loved spending time with Zoe and seeing the world through her young eyes, so I didn't care why she was spending time with me. Although it would have been nice if she'd said she liked my stimulating company and not just my quiet flat.

Of course, being a teenager, Zoe wasn't always delightful. There were some evenings when I was more than grateful to take her back to Karen after an hour or so. But they were few and far between. On the whole, I just loved having her company.

Karen and I were forty the year Zoe turned sixteen.

'Do you remember when we were that age?' Karen asked, before we spent the rest of the evening laughing about the crazy things we did in our teens.

'I don't feel forty,' she admitted at one point.

'Neither do I, at least not on the inside, but I'm seriously thinking of changing my car,' I confessed. 'Those low sport's seats are starting to give me back problems.'

Since I'd return to the Southampton office, I'd started seeing a lot of Seb. I wasn't sure if it was being forty, but for the first time I felt settled and happy in a relationship.

It was on my forty-second birthday that Seb proposed to me. Even I was shocked when I said yes.

'So does that mean you'll now have children?' Zoe asked.

'Don't be silly, I'm too old and besides you know I can't stand kids.'

'That's just not true, look how you've always been with me.'

'You're different,' I pointed out. 'But remember, I couldn't even stand you as a baby. You were smelly and cried all the time.'

'Rubbish, I was a perfect baby. Irresistible then and irresistible now. Gotta love me,' Zoe laughed, as she flung her not so chubby arms around my neck. Then she added in a much more serious voice, 'Leah, I think you'd make a lovely mum.'

Which, for some stupid reason, made me want to cry.

For Zoe's eighteenth birthday, I splashed out and bought her a little car. I was sure it would be the last meaningful present I'd buy her, because surely now that she'd left school, she really wouldn't have time to spend with me.

I was sort of right, because I didn't see as much of her. But I was delighted that she seemed to want to stay in touch. She still came and visited me, and about once a month we had dinner together. Zoe would keep me up to date on her love life, although I found it hard trying to remember all the boys' names.

'Now you know how I used to feel with all your boyfriends,' Karen said one day over a cup of coffee. 'I have a feeling my daughter is taking after you more than she is me. See nurture does beat nature.'

'You think I've influenced Zoe?' I gasped.

'Of course you've influenced her.'

'In a bad way?'

'Oh, Leah, you should see your face.' Karen laughed. 'Of course I didn't mean in a bad

A Lack of Maternal Instinct

way. But you've been a big part of her life, you're important to her.'

Was I? I knew she was important to me, and I felt truly blessed that the feeling might be mutual. Perhaps I'd underestimated the power of those bedtime cuddles just after she'd lost her dad. I'd only given them because I didn't know what else to do. Maybe they'd forged a bond far deeper than I'd ever realised.

Zoe was twenty-seven when she walked down the aisle. She looked so beautiful.

'How did she get to be this grown up,' I whispered to Seb as we sat in the church. Surely, it was just yesterday I'd been reading her those bedtime stories.

'Are you sorry she's not your daughter?' he asked, as we stood to one side watching them take the family photos.

I looked over at Karen in all her finery. She was standing there looking so proud of Zoe. Did I wish that was me instead of her? Not a chance.

'Have you any idea how much hassle Karen has had over this wedding,' I exclaimed.

I'd bought the happy couple a nice wedding present and I'd contributed to the cost of the

A Lack of Maternal Instinct

reception, but I wasn't daft, I'd kept well away from the panic and arguments that seemed to surround organising the event. Although that didn't mean I wasn't delighted when Zoe called me over.

'We've got to have a photo of me standing between you and Mum,' she said, draping a lace-covered arm around each of us. Then she added as we smiled for the camera, 'Thank you both so much, not just for today but for everything.'

I looked at Karen, and she looked at me. Terrific! As if we weren't tearful enough already.

I was sad when Zoe and her husband moved off the Island, but luckily it wasn't that far away, and she often come back to visit. I was thrilled that those visits usually included seeing me.

I was fifty-six when Zoe gave birth to a daughter and Karen proudly showed me the photos.

'Isn't she the most beautiful grandchild you've ever seen?'

I looked at the photos for a while before smiling at her.

'She's the image of her mother at that age,' I replied. As in, she was small, red and wrinkly, but I decided not to add that.

Freya was four weeks old when I met her. Zoe tried to get me to hold her.

'No, I'd rather not. I might break her,' I said backing away.

'Oh, Leah,' she laughed. 'You never change do you.' Which was a nice thing to say considering I was now as wrinkly as the baby.

'Have you ever regretted not being a mother?' she asked as she started to do something disgusting with a nappy.

'No, never,' I said.

'That's what I thought. But I still think you'd have made a good one, which is why I'd like you to be Freya's godmother.'

I just stared at Zoe for a moment, then I stared at the baby. What could I say? Me, a godmother?

'Don't worry,' Zoe said giving me a hug. 'I promise I won't ask you to babysit until she's toilet trained.'

'Oh, Zoe,' was all I could manage.

I'd never wanted to be a mother, not even the lovely Zoe's, but a godmother, now that was a whole different ball game. After all, wasn't it a godmother's job to bring joy and happiness into a little girl's life? And didn't godmothers leave the messier and less pleasant aspects of child rearing to those better suited for such tasks?

Of course they did. And, with my lack of maternal instinct, I knew this was a role I was perfectly qualified to fulfil.

Flying Free

With an impressive show of strength, Adrian effortlessly placed the owl box at Trish's feet.

'It's big, isn't it,' she said, wondering how of earth she was supposed to get that halfway up a large tree.

'I hope Derek will be helping you,' Adrian said.

Trish shifted uncomfortably before giving a half-hearted nod. What were the chances of Derek lifting a finger to help? Somewhere between none at all and not a lot, but she didn't want to admit that to Adrian.

So far no one in the village had indicated they knew her ratbag boyfriend was having an affair with Vicky, the barmaid at the local pub. But this was a small village, so Trish couldn't believe it was still a secret. Although she doubted that Vicky's husband knew, or perhaps he didn't care.

She watched as Adrian got back into his van and drove away. She really did appreciate him making this new home for her beautiful barn owl, but she had no idea if Barnie would have the sense to use it.

As far as Trish knew, the owl had started living in the old ash tree just after they'd moved into the cottage. She hadn't seen him for the first four weeks, then suddenly he was around all the time. She'd been thrilled. Now the poor old tree was going to have to be chopped down, and she was devastated.

It was odd, but the ash tree and her relationship with Derek seemed to start dying about the same time. Yet both had looked so healthy at the beginning.

Trish had met Derek while she was holidaying on the Isle of Wight. In just ten days she'd fallen head over heels in love with him, the Island, and with Joanna, Derek's mum. Her own parents were in the midst of a messy divorce and the company she worked for were starting to make redundancies, it felt like her whole world was falling apart. Which probably explains why she'd jumped at the chance of a little happiness when it was offered to her.

Lisa, the friend she'd travelled with, had tried to slow her down, as had her family when she returned home, but she hadn't listened.

At first she tried visiting Derek every other weekend, but that was both time consuming and expensive. His excuse for not visiting her was that he had to work late on Fridays, whereas she finished at two and could get to the Island by late evening, giving them all day Saturday and Sunday morning together. WhatsApp messages and calls kept them going the rest of the time, but it wasn't a great way to conduct a love affair.

When it was finally Trish's turn to receive the redundancy notice, Derek had suggested she move over to the Island to be with him. She'd jumped at the chance.

Joanna had made her feel so welcome in her home, and everything seemed to fall into place. Living with Derek was everything she'd dreamed it would be, and she'd found a great job very quickly. Island life suited her just fine. But, after a while, she felt that staying with Joanna

Flying Free

wasn't right. Living on her generosity was too much of an imposition.

Then her boss mentioned that he had a little place he rented out, and that it was about to become vacant. Was she interested? Was she ever. It was just like one of those rose covered cottages you see on the telly.

Derek complained that it needed decorating, but she'd pointed out that she was getting it at a reduced rent, and besides she enjoyed painting. Which was possibly why he'd left all the decorating to her. He also left her to furnish the place, saying he had terrible taste, and knew she'd make a much better job of turning it into a home without his input.

At the time she thought it was great he trusted her so much. Funny how you could mistake apathy for kindness when you had rose-coloured glasses covering your eyes.

The garden was one of the things she so loved about the cottage, especially the ash tree at the bottom of the long, dandelion covered lawn. It marked the boundary between the house and the neighbouring field, and its branches glowed bright crimson when the sun glowed behind it.

Flying Free

Then, a month after moving in, she'd been amazed to see this barn owl poking around the trunk.

The tree surgeon had recently told her that even back then the heart of the ash would have been dying. But it wasn't until this spring that she noticed something was wrong. Hardly any of the ash's leaves unfurled, and Derek started rolling home later and later. Sometimes with his clothes crumpled and reeking of perfume.

The tree and Derek's love seemed inexplicably linked. Trish tried so many things, but nothing she did could stop either of them from withering away. If the tree surgeon was right, there was nothing she could have done to save the ash. Was the same true about Derek? Had he ever really loved her?

In the early days it had seemed so, except now she could look back and see the odd telltale signs. Oh yes, she'd amused him at the start, he'd liked the cottage once she'd got it organised, and was even interested in Barnie for a short time.

They would sit in the bay window watching as the barn owl poked his head out of his hole. The bird would edge his way slowly towards the outer branches before suddenly spreading his wings and lifting high into the sky.

Trish had never seen a wild owl before and she'd been fascinated watching it criss-cross the fields early in the mornings. It was magical seeing him hover then dive to catch his breakfast.

She wasn't sure when she named him Barnie, or when she started going to the bottom of the garden to talk to him, but he'd become a very important part of her life. Even now she still got a thrill seeing him gliding overhead.

Derek on the other hand was easily bored. First it was by Barnie, then by the cottage, then finally it was her. So why didn't he move out? Was it because his new girlfriend was married and staying where he was provided a convenient cover?

Over the last month Trish had spent hours sitting under the ash tree telling Barnie her problems. With his head cocked to one side, it did seem like he was listening. Wisely, he didn't offer useless advice or complain when she cried.

She looked at Barnie's new home and with a show of over-optimistic determination, she tried to lift it. She got it a little way off the ground then it slipped and gave her a nasty big splinter.

Flying Free

Somehow, she had to get it across the garden, through the gap in the fence, into the field and twenty foot up a tree. The farmer had told her he was happy to have Barnie in residence, but he hadn't offered any assistance. And, of course, Trish wanted it up the highest tree so she could still see it from the house. If she couldn't talk to Barnie in the future, she still wanted to watch him, assuming he liked his new home.

'What the hell's this?' Derek demanded when he walked in from work.

'It's the new owl box for Barnie. The tree surgeon says it should be in place at least a month before the ash is cut down.'

'And how's that dumb bird supposed to know he's got to move? Are you going to send him an eviction notice?' Derek gave a scornful laugh before grabbing a beer and plonking himself in front of the telly.

'Before Barnie can move,' she said twenty minutes later as she handed Derek his dinner, 'someone has to climb the tree and put the owl box in place,'

'Well, don't look at me,' he snapped, grabbing the tomato ketchup.

She'd guessed that would be his response, but she had hoped.

Having lost her appetite, she left Derek to his meal and walked out into the garden. She was only just holding back the tears as she made her way to the ash tree. The nights were starting to draw in and the air felt damp, but she could still smell the scent of the last of the roses.

She looked up and saw Barnie perched on one of the outer branches. There wasn't anything she could do to save her relationship with Derek, not that she wanted to any longer, but she did want to help Barnie.

'How do I get your new house up a tree? And how do I convince you to move into it?'

He did nothing but shut one eye. They watched each other for a while, then she walked back to the house. She was sure Derek hadn't noticed she'd left.

'I'll ring Adrian,' she said. 'Maybe he'll know someone who'll help me put up the box.'

Derek grunted something without taking his eyes off the TV screen. She didn't bother finding out what.

Flying Free

'I'll bring Dad with me, and we'll fix it. Is four on Friday afternoon okay?' Adrian asked, when Trish rang him.

She left work early that day and stood by the old ash watching Adrian and his dad haul the box up the farmer's tree. She told Barnie all about his new home, and although she couldn't actually see him, she hoped he was listening.

Half an hour later the box was in place. She made some coffee, and they all sat in her kitchen watching to see what Barnie would do. Needless to say, he did nothing.

'It's early days,' Adrian said reassuringly, after they'd been chatting for an hour and Barnie hadn't even stuck his beak outside his hole.

'What will happen if he's still in the tree when it gets cut down?' she asked.

'Don't worry, owls are resourceful birds. Barnie will find himself a new home.'

'I feel terrible about kicking him out,' she muttered.

'I think you should feel free to kick anything out of your home,' Adrian said pointedly. Then he added, 'If you ever need anything Trish, you know where I am.'

They left as soon as Derek's van pulled up outside.

'I'm off out,' Derek announced after he'd changed into a clean shirt. 'I'll be late back.'

'Of course you will.'

A short while later, Trish sat at her computer and typed a letter.

Dear Barnie,

I'm so sorry but I have to give you four weeks' notice to quit your home. Despite my best efforts I couldn't save your tree but, as a responsible landlord, I have provided you with alternative accommodation. I hope you will move in and be happy there.

I'm going to miss you.
Lots of love,
Trish x

She printed it out, slipped it in a plastic folder and took it down to the bottom of the garden. The ladder Adrian had used was still out, so she carefully placed it against the tree, climbed up to the lowest of the branches that Barnie used and pinned up the letter. She did know that most people would think she was crazy but really, what was wrong with doing crazy things on occasions?

Trish climbed back down, put the ladder away in the shed and walked back to the cottage. Once there she grabbed her mobile and made a difficult call.

Two hours later, she sat down again at her computer and typed another letter.

Derek,

I'm sorry our relationship has failed, but I think you'll agree that you leaving is best for both of us.

I've told your mum all about your married girlfriend, and she's agreed that you can move back in with her until you get yourself sorted. She is expecting you tonight.

Trish.

She printed it off and pinned it to one of the black sacks she'd just filled with Derek's clothes and personal belongings. Then she dragged the lot out onto the drive ready for when he finally rolled home.

Flying Free

Joanna had been very understanding, and had even hinted that she was surprised Trish had put up with her son for so long.

'Oh Trish, I hope we can still be friends,' she said at the end of the call. Then she asked if the two of them could meet up for a coffee the following week.

Trish was relieved and very happy. She'd assumed she'd lose Joanna along with Derek.

With everything dumped out on the drive, Trish slipped the safety chain in place on the door, making sure Derek couldn't get back in. Then she turned out the lights and went to bed.

Eight weeks later and Adrian was helping her plant an apple tree in the space left by the ash.

'It's wonderful that Barnie's settled in the box,' he said, as they stood watching the bird glide across the field.

'I think he appreciated all that soft bedding you put in for him,' she replied.

Barnie took two weeks to pack his wings and move. Derek had simply loaded his stuff into his van that night and left.

He had come back a week later for some tools from the shed and to give her back his key.

He'd said he was sorry it hadn't worked out, but he hadn't looked sorry.

It was funny but, despite it being winter, the place seemed brighter now. The cottage felt warmer and the garden lighter. Perhaps it was because the big tree had gone, or maybe it was because no one was casting a dark shadow over her.

Everyone had been so supportive since Derek had left, especially Adrian. For some reason, he kept dropping round to make sure the owl box was okay. And, to show him just how much she appreciated his help, Trish had invited him to stay for dinner that evening.

'So, when do you think I'll get my first apple pie?' Adrian asked as he looked down at the little twig-sized tree poking out of the ground.

'My best guess would be at least five years. I hope you aren't hungry,' she laughed.

'I reckon I can wait that long,' he replied, grinning in a way that lit up his whole face.

With that, Barnie swooped down and landed on her fence. He'd done that a few times now and hadn't flown away when she'd gone out and talked to him. She couldn't help thinking she was grateful that it was Derek who'd disappeared from her life and not the owl.

'You know Barnie could be female don't you,' Adrian said. 'I was reading that if we put up a second box close by, we might get a breeding pair.'

Trish's heart gave a little flutter, the "we" in the sentence sounded promising. Then he'd smiled and taken hold of her hand as they walked back to the cottage.

This time round she had no intention of rushing into anything but maybe, like the apple tree, this relationship would grow and blossom over time.

Surprise Surprise!

After thirty-five years of marriage, it wasn't hard to tell when my husband was up to something. Dan had always loved to surprise me by organising parties, nights out and presents, but he was useless at hiding his excitement while planning such things. He'd develop a glint in his eye, wear an all-knowing grin and start whistling. It was a dead giveaway. He was also hopeless at covering his tracks, so I always found out his "surprise" long before the event. Not that I ever ruined his fun by telling him this.

And I hadn't told him this time either, but I'd recently found all the campervan brochures that he'd supposedly hidden. And, of all the "surprises" he'd pulled over the years, this had to be the worst idea ever.

'Well, that's it, Mandy,' Dan said cheerfully, as he walked into the kitchen covered in creosote. 'Next door is completely finished. I've fixed and painted the last fence panel, so we are now officially two separate properties.'

'It'll seem odd,' I admitted, as I switched on the kettle in my gleaming new kitchen.

'I know, but it'll be great when it completes on Friday. We can hand over the keys to the new owners and pay off the bank. I can't say I'm sorry because it's been hard work.' Then Dan grinned, his eyes shining. 'But it's been worth the effort, Mandy. We can now get on with our lives.'

I listened as Dan whistled his way to the bathroom, he was so happy. How could I tell him that, thanks to his "surprise", my future wasn't feeling so great.

We'd run the village shop for thirty-two years, which meant we'd never had time for proper holidays. I'd always dreamed of buying a little place by the sea when we retired, and Dan had always said he wanted to tour around the country. Stupidly, we'd believed we'd have the money to do both. Only life hadn't turned out the way we planned.

Running the shop had been fun in the early days. So many of the locals had used us that we'd been able to afford to employ someone to cover for us if we wanted a few days off. But as the years went by it became harder and harder. We'd ended up having to open the shop twelve hours a day, seven days a week just to make a profit.

With so little time off, wasn't it natural that we'd often sit and talk about the time when we'd be able to sell up and relax. We both dreamed of the day when we'd have no heavy boxes to lug around, no enormous freezers to clean, no endless paperwork to deal with, and especially no awkward customers demanding the impossible.

I pictured a life of long summer walks along a seashore, and winters in front of cosy open fires listening to the sound of waves crashing on the beach. As dreams went, it was perfect. Reality, of course, was anything but.

We'd always lived in the flat above the shop, and had always assumed our business was a valuable asset. But then they built the big supermarket down the road and, at the same time, we'd had to compete with things like online shopping and home delivery services. Suddenly our little business was losing money.

Oh, the locals made more effort once they realised we were thinking of closing, but buying the odd carton of milk or half a dozen stamps from us just wasn't enough. So nearly three years ago, with our overdraft increasing daily, we'd sadly hung the closed sign on the door before the bank did it for us.

With the date we could retire getting further away not closer, we'd taken the first jobs we could, which ironically were with the supermarket who'd put us out of business. But even with full time jobs, our debts meant we were still struggling to make ends meet.

Even with the shop empty, it was still costing us money, and no one was pounding on our door wanting to buy it. We loved living where we did, but ours wasn't the sort of village that Londoners paid a fortune to flock to at weekends. We didn't have a pub, or a community hall. There wasn't an attractive pond or even a tiny stream running by, and we certainly didn't have thatched cottages.

I could still remember the time Dan tried to grow roses around the shop door. All that happened was our customers complained about the greenfly.

Finally, we did get an offer from a builder, but he wanted the whole building, including our flat. His idea was to turn the place back into two semi-detached houses. Which was what the building had originally been long before we bought it.

'It's a ridiculously low offer,' Dan had ranted at the time. 'After we've paid off our overdraft, we won't have enough money to buy ourselves anything decent, at least not without a hefty mortgage.'

I'd looked at the figures, then sobbed for an hour because it seemed so unfair. All those years of long hours and hard work had amounted to nothing.

Or had it? Dan woke me in the middle of the night.

'Why can't we do the conversion ourselves Mandy?' he cried excitedly. 'You know I'm really good at DIY, so if I do most of the work, we can keep one of the houses to live in and sell off the other.'

We spent the next few weeks pricing it up, before talking to the bank to see if they'd lend us even more money. On paper it looked good, yet I was terrified of the risk we were taking. What if we messed it up? Trouble was, what other option did we have?

For two years now we've lived with brick dust, dirt and trailing wires, all while working full time. Every minute of our spare time was spent on the conversion. Dan dealt with everything bar the electrics, while I sorted out getting us the materials at the best prices possible, plus I split the back into two gardens and did almost all the decorating. It was exhausting.

However, we now had a very nice house of our own, even though it felt strange going upstairs to bed after all the years of living in a flat. We'd even managed to sell the second semi for more than we expected. It was enough to clear our debts and leave a nice amount in the bank. Or I hoped it did, but that rather depended on how much Dan had spent on his stupid surprise.

One of the advantages of working for someone else was getting paid holidays. We'd arranged to take two weeks of our annual leave starting on Friday. The day next door completed.

At first, I'd assumed we'd sit down together and plan where to go, but no, Dan had decided he wanted to "surprise" me. And if my husband thought a campervan was the sort of "surprise" that would thrill me, he was very wrong. I still dreamed of my cottage by the sea, but as that wasn't going to be possible, then two weeks by a nice beach would be a reasonable compromise. I'd be happy staying in a nice Airbnb or even a little hotel, anything really as long as it wasn't in some poky dolls house on wheels.

I was upset that Dan had done this without consulting me, yet I could tell he thought it was a fantastic idea, and he'd always wanted to travel the country. Something I'd once thought sounded great. But that was when I'd assumed we'd have a nice comfortable car to travel in. Not to mention my dislike these days of long traffic jams, and my aging and less than perfect bladder. Hmm, let's not mention that.

Dan was obviously excited by the thought of a campervan, but after all these years together you'd have thought he'd have known the idea wouldn't excite me. I thought he knew me better.

Several times over the last couple of weeks I'd been tempted to tell him this, only he'd worked so hard time over the last few years, and it was great to see him smiling again. How could I ruin his plans? And, as my sister had pointed out, there was a chance I'd love living on the road in a tiny van. A very, very, very slim chance!

Finally, completion day arrived, and we helped our new neighbours move in. The money went into our account, and most of it went out again but for the first time in years we didn't owe the bank anything.

'Out of debt and on holiday, what could be better?' Dan said at the end of the day, before starting to whistle again.

I'd have been happy with a bottle of Champagne to celebrate, instead I had to pack a suitcase and pretend I was looking forward to Dan's "surprise."

I had tried to ask a few questions about it, but he'd just given me a hug and told me that all would soon be revealed. I still had no idea how to handle the situation. After all the years of worrying and working flat out, it felt wrong being grumpy now. And there was no way of telling from the pile of brochures I'd found which type of van he'd gone for. Although I

Surprise Surprise!

knew we didn't have the money for the more acceptable ones.

Saturday morning dawned bright and sunny, and we made an early start. We'd only been travelling for a few minutes when I worked out Dan was heading south.

'Can't you at least tell me our destination,' I said.

He stopped whistling.

'Well, I suppose that can't hurt now we're on our way. We're off to the Isle of Wight,' he said.

'Where we went on our honeymoon,' I gasped, suddenly feeling hopeful.

As a wedding present, my grandparents had paid for us to stay in a guesthouse in Cowes. That had been the longest holiday Dan and I had ever taken together, and we'd spent some of the time playing in boats and learning to sail a bit. It had been fantastic. It was when our dream of living by the sea had first begun.

'You never said this was going to be a second honeymoon,' I said, smiling a real smile for the first time today.

'I haven't said much about it,' he reminded me. 'And I'm not telling you anything else until we arrive, so stop asking,' he laughed, before starting to whistle again.

I certainly wasn't going to ask anymore. I was going to spend the whole journey fantasising that we'd be staying in a romantic hotel for the next ten days. Well, a woman could dream.

The journey was horrendous, which convinced me even more that being stuck in endless traffic jams was not my idea of fun, although I supposed having a loo onboard might help. I was so pleased when we finally drove onto the ferry. The crossing was relaxing as we sat outside and watched the boats.

We drove off the ferry just before noon, found a nice pub and stopped to get something to eat. We were halfway through a delicious ploughman's lunch, when I noticed Dan glance at his watch and start eating faster.

'Are you in a hurry for some reason?' I asked.

'We're due to meet someone at two,' he said.

'Are we? I don't suppose you'll tell me who?' I snapped.

'Jeffery Simmons,' he replied with a grin. 'But I'm still not telling you why.'

Surprise Surprise!

Dan hurriedly finished the rest of his food, but I'd rather lost my appetite. What was I going to do? Apart from clobber my husband when he started up that damned whistling again.

It took him thirty minutes and a couple of wrong turns, before he finally drove into a small car park.

'I think this is the place,' he said.

As I opened the car door, a man about our own age approached us.

'You must be Dan and Mandy,' he said. 'I'm Jeff. I hope you had a good journey over.'

He and Dan started chatting, and I started looking around for a van. This looked like some sort of marina, so there were boats and water and a few cars, but not a campervan in sight. Dan, with an even brighter glint in his eye, took my hand and gave it a squeeze.

'My surprise,' he whispered, as we followed Jeff down a jetty and onto a rather nice-looking sailing boat.

'She's thirty foot long, ten years old and has been well looked after,' Jeff explained to me. 'She can sleep six at a push but, to be honest, with boats this size it's far more comfortable if it's just the two of you.'

'So, what do you think?' Dan asked. 'I know it's not exactly the cottage we'd dreamed about, but you have to admit you can't get any closer to the sea.'

I just stared at him.

'It took me a while to find a decent boat we could afford,' he admitted. 'And if you like it, Jeff here is going to spend the next week teaching us to sail it.'

I turned to Jeff, who had the same silly grin on his face as my husband. Dan had never pulled off a surprise in his life, until now! I was completely gobsmacked.

'Please say something,' Dan begged. 'I haven't bought the boat yet, so if you really hate it we can go and find a hotel instead.'

A hotel… was he kidding?

'Oh Dan, I love it,' I gasped, as I flung my arms around him. 'It's perfect, but can we really afford it?'

'Trust me,' he whispered. 'We'll still have a nice amount left in the bank. And having this means all our future holidays and weekends away are sorted.'

With that idea in mind, I spent a while studying the kitchen area, it was well equipped for such a small space, and the sitting area was lovely. It even had a TV. The main bedroom had a nice sized bed with just enough room each side for us to get out, and there was a lot more cupboard space than one would imagine. The shower was tiny, but there were two loos. I couldn't stop smiling.

We then went back on deck and sat down. Suddenly it was easy picturing the sails up, the wind blowing, the water lapping around the bow and me sitting with a glass of wine in my hand. This was my idea of heaven, but my curiosity was getting to me.

'So, what happened to the campervan?'

Dan laughed as he slipped his arm around me. 'Just this once I wanted to surprise you. And I knew the only way I could do that was by letting you think you'd discovered what I was planning.' Then he added. 'I hope you aren't disappointed?'

The crafty old devil knew I wasn't disappointed.

This may not be my dreamed about cottage by the sea, but if I had to have a caravan sized something, then one floating on water suited me just fine.

Surprise Surprise!

'This is fantastic, thank you,' I sighed, as I leaned over to kiss him. That was when I noticed another glint in his eye. Oh my, maybe our second honeymoon would be even more fun than the first. Now wouldn't that be a surprise.

Acknowledgements

I'd like to thank my wonderful writing friends for all their much-appreciated encouragement over the years. Della Galton, Lin Mitchelmore and Jennifer Bohnet. What would I have done without you?

And a very special thanks to Teresa Ashby who has been my inspiration from the very start.

Also thanks to Jane, my life-long friend.

For their proofreading skills, I have to give a big thank you to Lin and to my dear friend Yvonne Hartstone.

And for teaching me publishing skills my thanks go to Diana and Steve Kimpton.

And last but not least, to the Mountbatten Hospice – I thank you so very much for the years of care you gave my friend Sue.

Printed in Great Britain
by Amazon